MY
FATHER'S WIFE
AND MY
DAUGHTER'S
EMU

To Alison,

With great appreciation!

Nina

MY FATHER'S WIFE AND MY DAUGHTER'S EMU

linked stories

Nina Dabek

atmosphere press

TABLE OF CONTENTS

Part I: The Past Makes Its Own Future

Part II: And Love Promises More Love

For Peggy, Nadja, and Eva

and also for Jan

PART I

THE PAST MAKES ITS OWN FUTURE

YOM KIPPUR AT THE ZOO

When I was seven we went to the Bronx Zoo on Yom Kippur. My sisters had gone with my mother to wait in line for a camel ride, but I hadn't wanted to—too bumpy. Instead, I went with my father to look at the elephants. We were all going to meet afterwards at the snack bar, and get an ice cream. My father and I stood in front of the elephants' cage with a bag of peanuts. The slats of the cage were far enough apart to allow the elephant trunks to reach through them. It was a crisp October day and although we were outside, the rank smell of the elephants burned in my nose. I poured a few peanuts into my hand and tentatively held it out, palm flat, as I knew to do, brushing my arm lightly against my father's brown corduroy jacket, which hung open.

My father was fasting, and I remember thinking that maybe I wouldn't get an ice cream, because maybe it would be hard for my father to sit with us while we were eating our cones. Three elephants, trunks dancing in the air like antennae, crowded near the fence close to a group

3

of people. Then the biggest of the three ambled with heavy steps over to where we stood. I drew my hand back a couple of inches.

My father's voice was lively. "It's coming toward you, Naomi. Look, it smells the peanuts. It's hungry—it wants to eat them." Other people have told me my father speaks with an accent, but I have never heard it.

The elephant had big black eyes. Its wrinkled grey skin was covered with dirt and straw and I could see a small insect crawling down its forehead toward the corner of one big, blinking eye. The trunk looked pink inside, wet and gooey. I wasn't sure I wanted it to touch me. I pulled my hand away from the outstretched trunk.

"What's the matter?" my father said. "Are you scared? There's nothing to be scared of."

I wanted him to go first, but I wasn't sure he could feed the elephant if he wasn't eating himself. I wasn't sure if he could even touch food. "Daddy, are you allowed to give food to the elephant? On Yom Kippur?"

He burst out in laughter. "What, you think this elephant is observant?" He reached his hand out toward the elephant's trunk as though to pat it. Sunlight reflected off his plain gold wedding band. The elephant pulled its trunk back with a little snort. My father snorted back. "He's not stupid. He doesn't want my hand, he wants those peanuts." He took the bag from me and poured a few peanuts into his own hand. "Okay, here you go, you want some food?" He stretched his open palm out toward the elephant.

The elephant moved its trunk back and forth and finally landed on my father's hand, sucking up the peanuts and then reaching toward the rest of the bag. My father

4

pulled the bag away and stepped back. "*Chazer*," he laughed. "*Shvignac*." I watched the elephant loop its trunk around to place the peanuts in its mouth.

My father poured a few more peanuts into his hand. "This is a hungry one," he said to me. "Do you want to try? Should we do it together?" Together we stretched our hands out, held them, palms flat, within reach of the elephant. The elephant once again waved its trunk in the air as it drew closer. I wanted to pull back, but I kept my arm close to my father's. In one motion the elephant swooped across first my hand, then my father's, vacuumed up the peanuts and deposited them in its mouth, then came back searching for more. The trunk had been wet inside, with small bristles that tickled my palm.

"More?" said my father. "Do you want to do it yourself this time?" But I liked doing it with him, so together we fed the elephant over and over again until the bag of peanuts was empty.

"Okay," he said, crumpling the bag in one hand, and looking around for a garbage can. "Let's go meet your mother and Leah and Rachel. Are you hungry? Ready for an ice cream?"

"Are you hungry, Daddy?"

My father laughed. "I'm a little hungry."

"Why can't you eat?"

"Well, I fast on Yom Kippur out of respect for your grandmother." His mother had died when I was four. She died of colon cancer, but I was always confused about whether her death also had something to do with the war. His family had come over from France during World War II when he was still a boy.

"Are you allowed to drink?"

"Not until dinnertime." He looked at his watch. "Another couple of hours."

I wanted to ask him more questions, but I thought it might make him sad to think about his mother, so I didn't say anything. We walked hand-in-hand over to the snack bar. Leah and Rachel were already sitting at a round metal table with my mother, licking their cones, while my mother sipped on a straw from a big paper cup.

"Here they come. What kind of ice cream do you want?" asked my mother, as we approached the table and sat down. She pulled a couple of packets of individually wrapped Wash'n Dris out of her pocketbook and handed one to my father before opening the other for me. "If you've been feeding the elephants, you should wipe your hands."

"I don't really want any ice cream," I said.

"No ice cream? Are you sure? How were the elephants? Do you want something else? Something to drink?" She reached out for my hand and wiped it front and back with the Wash'n Dri, then did the same with my other hand.

"No, thanks. I don't really want anything."

"The ice cream's really good," Rachel said as she waved her chocolate cone under my nose. "Chocolate. Your favorite."

"Mine's vanilla," Leah said. "Yummy."

"I don't want anything," I said.

I watched my father as he tore open his Wash'n Dri packet, scraped at the little wet cloth to unfold it, and wiped his hands methodically, first front and back, then each finger separately, even under his nails. I looked down at my hands. Were they clean? I couldn't really tell. The

Wash'n Dri my mother had used for me was lying on the table. I picked it up and began to wipe my fingers in the same way that he did. My father knows the right way to do things.

THE FIRE

The early evening sun distorted our shadows as we wheeled our bicycles down the long ramp that turned a sharp corner, twice, to make a concrete "Z" leading from the street to the heavy steel doors of the building's basement. Inside it was dank and musty, the only light filtering through dirty windows spaced far apart. Rows and rows of electrical meters lined the gray walls, each with a curved glass cover protecting the little clocks underneath. There were over a hundred of them, one for each apartment. My mother had warned us not to touch the meters. She said they carried a strong electric current and if we touched them we would receive a shock, a dangerous shock.

My older sister Rachel didn't believe her. "Those glass covers protect you from the current," she said. "Nothing will happen if you touch one. Go ahead, try it." We stood with our bikes, waiting for the elevator. I would not touch one. I didn't know whether my mother was right or Rachel, but why risk it?

My mother had told us to be sure to be back by five-thirty, and we were late. She was planning an early dinner because she was hoping to go out afterwards with my father to buy some new wallpaper for the kitchen. My mother always had ambitions for our apartment. This would be the first time my parents left the three of us—Rachel, my younger sister Leah, and me—at home alone after dark.

Rachel and I had biked over to the field behind P.S. 24, where the Little League played. She had a crush on Joel Epstein, the pitcher. She didn't want to go by herself to watch him pitch because she didn't want to seem obvious about it, so she had asked me if I would bike over with her. I liked watching baseball. I would have liked to play, but girls weren't allowed in the Little League.

"Okay, if you're not going to try it, I will," Rachel said and reached a hand out toward one of the electrical meters while she steadied her bike with her other hand.

"Rachel, don't," I screamed. "Don't touch it, you don't know." I imagined Rachel all lit up from the current, falling to the ground in pain, maybe dead. "You'll get a shock. Mommy said not to touch it." If Rachel touched the meter and then let go of her bicycle from the shock, and Rachel's bicycle fell over and touched mine, would the current pass through and I would get the shock too and also die? Rachel laughed, she let her finger come within a quarter-inch of the glass cover, but she didn't touch it. Why wouldn't the elevator come?

I heard the sound of the steel basement door scraping open, and a triangle of light lit the floor. Four girls in gray and black plaid jumpers—uniforms from St. Gabriel's, the Catholic school across the street—clattered through the doorway. I recognized one of them; she lived in an apartment on the seventh floor.

The elevator doors opened just as the girls approached, laughing about something. "Not bubble gum!" one of them shrieked, and they laughed harder. Rachel wheeled her bike into the elevator. I started to follow her, but my bike began to tip over as I let go with one hand in order to hold onto the elevator button so the doors wouldn't close. The biggest girl crowded behind me.

"Sorry," I said. "I don't think everybody will fit. I mean, with our bikes. Maybe you could wait till it comes back down? Sorry."

She stepped back, made a big bubble with her gum and let it pop, sucking it back into her mouth before she spoke. "I guess if we have to wait..."

I let my finger drop from the elevator button. If only they would stop looking at me. My bike tipped at a precarious angle against the closing doors. Rachel managed to reach the "door open" button inside the elevator and when she pressed it the doors popped open with a jerk. The sudden release from the hold of the elevator doors sent my bike toppling toward me, knocking me over. I thought I felt my fingers brush against one of the glass covers and I screamed. The four girls started to laugh. Inside the elevator, Rachel also started to laugh as she continued to press the "door open" button.

Had I gotten an electrical shock? It didn't seem like it. I disentangled myself from my bike, stood up, and managed to wheel the bike into the elevator. The girl with the bubble gum unclasped and reclasped her barrette as the elevator doors closed. "Stupid bikes," she called out at the last minute.

"Why did you laugh?" I asked Rachel. "You shouldn't have laughed." I noticed a scrape on my arm, but otherwise I wasn't hurt.

"You looked so funny when your bike kept falling, and then when you fell and screamed..."

"I think Mommy was wrong about the meters," I said.

"Did you really touch one of the meters? No wonder you screamed."

"I'm pretty sure I did. Should we tell her?"

"Not if you're not sure." Rachel was definite.

"Yeah, maybe not." I twisted my arm to look more closely at the scrape. "That girl was so mean."

"Yeah, calling us stupid kikes."

"Stupid kikes? What's that? I thought she said 'stupid bikes.'"

"No, she said 'stupid kikes.' It means Jews."

"It does? She said that?" I knew that some people didn't like Jews. I knew about the Holocaust because my father and his family had escaped during the war—but I didn't ever think that someone would say something like that to me.

"Yeah. She said that. But don't tell Daddy. It would upset him."

The elevator came to a lurching halt and the doors opened. I smelled something inviting. Was it fried chicken for dinner? I hoped the smell was coming from our apartment. We got our bikes out without difficulty. Before the doors began to close, I reached inside the elevator and pressed as many buttons as I could.

When dinner was almost over—it *was* fried chicken—my mother brought up the subject of the wallpaper. My father did not want to spend money. He didn't think we had the money to spend. But the old wallpaper, little bouquets of blue and green flowers on a white background, was starting to fray at the edges. It had gotten greasy and you couldn't really wash off that grease anymore. It made the flowers look wilted and even moldy, the way dead flowers scum up in a vase. My mother had mentioned the wallpaper every night that week. Now she said, "Ella Sachs told me there's a new kind of wallpaper—she just bought some—that's easy to hang. No glue, nothing. We can hang it ourselves. She even offered to help me hang it. And it's inexpensive. She told me what she paid. And think of the money we'll save on a babysitter!"

Ella lived in apartment 4M on the other side of our building. It was a huge apartment building: only seven stories high, but so wide it stretched all the way between two streets, with four different elevators. If you wanted to go to an apartment that wasn't in your wing, you had to go down to the lobby and walk across and take a different elevator.

"You're sure it's okay to leave the girls here by themselves?" asked my father. "It's getting dark already."

My mother said, "Rachel's twelve now and Leah and Naomi are old enough that we can leave them with her. It won't take more than an hour: the girls will be fine at home. They won't even have to get in their pajamas—we'll be that quick. Okay, Rachel?" My mother was spilling over with excitement at the thought of leaving us alone in the apartment to go buy new wallpaper.

Rachel didn't care. She gave an indifferent snort, "Sure, go ahead."

I knew what that meant. Rachel had a phone right in

her own room and with our parents gone that's where she would be, in her room on the phone, and it would be up to me to play with my younger sister, Leah, who was six. It seemed it was always up to me to play with her. And to help her if she needed something.

"That's fine, then." My mother was good at moving things along. Her favorite expression was, "If you want to get something done, give it to a busy person." She didn't even ask Leah and me how we felt about it, and she didn't care what my father thought. Now she pushed her chair back and stood up. "This is a momentous occasion. It marks a new stage in our family. There's ice cream in the freezer for you girls. I bought it as a special treat to have when we're gone."

"Ice cream! Hurray!" shouted Leah.

While I followed my mother and Rachel into my mother's room, Leah went to our room to start setting up her stuffed animals for a game of animal shelter. She had gone to the shelter that afternoon with her best friend Isaac and his mother to help him pick out a cat, and she couldn't wait to start playing. It was a problem I had with Leah, that she always wanted me to play with her and if I said I didn't want to she would start to whine. I hated when she whined. Rachel never seemed to feel a responsibility to play with either one of us.

My mother had refreshed her lipstick and now as she rummaged in her closet for her other shoe, she spelled out for Rachel what to do in case something bad happened while they were gone. My mother used a particular perfume—Ma Griffe eau de toilette—and all her clothes smelled of it. With her closet door open I could smell it as I stood there. I loved that smell. Sometimes when my mother was not home, I would go into her closet, close the door, and just stand there breathing in that smell.

She was having trouble finding the one shoe she needed amongst the mess of shoes piled on the floor. She could never find the right one to match what she wanted. As she threw her shoes around she kept explaining: who to call if one of us got hurt, never to turn on the oven or stove, what to do if someone we didn't know rang the doorbell or called on the phone. Rachel stood behind my mother, examining her split ends and saying unh-hunh the way she does when she's not really listening. Her mind was probably on the long phone call to her best friend Linda that she was going to make just as soon as our parents had left. I didn't know what they ever talked about for so long. Probably today it would be that pitcher, Joel, but how much was there to say about him? I stood there, just in case my mother said something someone ought to pay attention to. It would really be up to me.

She finally found the shoe. My father was finishing up the dishes. His sleeves were rolled up and he had a little blue-and-white-checked dishtowel tucked in at his waist so that nothing would splash on his pants.

"Harry, what are you doing? The dishes can wait, we need to get going." He turned off the faucet and carefully dried his hands on the towel, hanging it neatly over the back of a chair on his way to join her in the hallway. As he rolled his sleeves back down, my mother looked at the towel and said, "We'll have to get new dishtowels, too, depending on what wallpaper we choose." I could see how happy it made her—the prospect of buying new items to match the new wallpaper. My father concentrated on snapping his cufflinks back in place.

Rachel and I followed my mother down the hallway to the front door. "Leah, we're leaving," my mother called out. "Come say goodbye."

"Goodbye," Leah called out from our bedroom. Rachel didn't wait for my mother to finish putting on her coat. She said good-bye and walked into her room, which was across the hallway from Leah's and mine, and closed her door.

"Do you have to go?" I asked my mother.

"We'll only be an hour. You'll be fine. Lock the door behind us," she said. "Double-lock it and put the chain on as well."

My father joined her in the front hall.

"How will you get back in if the chain is on?" I asked.

"Don't worry—we'll be home in an hour—you'll still be awake," my mother replied. "You can unlock it for us. Oh, and I forgot to tell Rachel—the phone list is in the kitchen by the phone. In case you need to call someone. Tell her to call Ella first."

"And don't open the door to a stranger," said my father.

"Don't open the door to anyone, period," my mother trumped him. "Until we get back. You never know."

"Alright, okay." I waited until they had rounded the corner and were out of sight before I closed the door, double locking it and putting the chain on.

In the bedroom that I shared with Leah, I sat down on the floor, leaning against my bed. I had only recently switched rooms—I used to share a bedroom with Rachel, but she was never very friendly, and she often made rules about when I was allowed to be in the room, even though it was my room too. There was only one fun thing she would do with me and that was at night sometimes after we went to bed we would play a game called "Little Sister" while we lay in our beds in the dark. In the game we were twins, always about nine or ten years old, and we had a lot of younger brothers and sisters. Our parents were dead, or maybe our mother was still alive but extremely sick, so it was up to us to take care of all the younger children, and we were poverty-stricken and sometimes didn't have a place to live. We always had to make sure that no grown-up would see us because if someone did they might separate us.

But Rachel stopped playing even that game with me, and Leah really wanted to be in a room with somebody, so a few months ago I moved into Leah's room. Our room still had the same wallpaper she had picked when it was all hers—zoo animals in shades of orange and yellow: lions and giraffes and monkeys on a white background. Leah had had a thing about animals for as long as I could remember.

Now she was trying to decide whether she could pass off her stuffed tiger as a cat in her animal shelter game. She had a lot of stuffed animals, but she didn't think all of them were suitable for the game. She was picking out the ones that were either dogs or cats or bunnies or looked as though we could pretend they were dogs or cats or bunnies. She spoke to each animal as she made her decision, holding it up close so that her lips brushed against the fur as she spoke. I couldn't hear the words. Sometimes I was struck with a warm feeling for Leah. It was just this kind of thing, whispering to her stuffed animals in a nice way as though they could understand her, that made me feel that way. I watched her do this until she was finished. I could hear the occasional shriek of laughter coming from Rachel's room. Leah looked up, ready to start the game.

"I'm the woman at the shelter." She gave me my instructions: "You're a mother who comes to the shelter to pick out an animal for your daughter as a surprise for her because you know she loves animals."

"Can I have two daughters?"

"Okay, but this is going to be a pet for the younger daughter."

"Won't the older daughter feel upset and resentful?"

"But that's the game. That's how I planned the game to be. The mother gives just one daughter an animal." The familiar whine started to creep into her voice.

"All right, we can do it your way, but you should know that the older daughter might be mean to the younger one when the mother gives her the pet."

I left the room, stared at Rachel's closed door, and then turned around and walked back in.

"Hello. I'm interested in a pet for my daughter. It's a surprise for her. She loves animals."

"Well, we have a lot of nice animals here that need a home. Would your daughter like a dog or a cat or a bunny?"

Just then the doorbell rang. I waited for Rachel to come out of her room and answer the door.

"Maybe Mommy and Daddy are back already," said Leah.

There were some loud knocks on the door. I could hear the faint buzz of the doorbell ringing in our next-door neighbor's apartment.

"Rachel should get the door. She's supposed to be in charge." I walked over to Rachel's room and shouted at her door, "Rachel, someone's at the front door."

"I'm on the phone."

Leah followed me to the front door.

A gruff male voice said, "Fire department."

Fire department. "Rachel," I shouted. "Rachel, you better get off the phone. Come out here." I pulled a chair over to the door to take a look through the peephole. It was a man dressed like a fireman, all distorted from the peephole glass. He banged on our door once more with his fist.

"Anybody home?"

I didn't answer. We weren't supposed to talk to strangers. Was he really a fireman, or just dressed that way? Was he going to trick us into telling him our parents weren't home so that we'd open the door? What would he do to us, if we let him in?

"We're evacuating the building," he called out. "There's a fire in the J to N wing, in front. You should be okay here, but as a precautionary measure, we're emptying the building. Thank you for your cooperation." I could see him walk away from the door.

"What is he saying?" asked Leah.

I was already at Rachel's door, knocking and kicking it open. "Rachel, you have to get off the phone, there's a fire."

Rachel sat on her bed, leaning against a blue corduroy pillow with armrests. She was just hanging up the phone. I sniffed the air, trying to smell smoke. I didn't smell anything.

"We're supposed to leave the building," I said.

"Is there a fire?" Leah asked, from where she stood

19

behind me.

"I guess so," I said, and sniffed again. There was no sign of a fire. Was there really a fire? Or was it some bad man trying to trick us? Rachel stood up.

"Maybe we should go out on the terrace..." I said. The terrace opened off my parents' bedroom. Our apartment was in the back of the building, and from there we wouldn't be able to see anything going on in the front of the building. But I was not ready yet to open the door and leave the apartment. I hoped that out on the terrace we would see something that would make it clear what we should do.

Outside the sky was a deepening twilight blue. Everything was still. Streetlamps lit the empty street. It was hard to imagine that there could be a fire anywhere in the building. I looked across the street toward the empty parking lot of St. Gabriel's Catholic school. We stood for a minute, and then I thought I smelled smoke, just a little bit. What if the fire spread to our apartment and we were trapped and had to jump from this terrace? It was a long way down. I couldn't imagine jumping.

"We should go," I said. "We should get out of here."

"Should we call Ella?" asked Rachel.

"I think we should just go."

"I'm going to call Ella. Mommy said call Ella if we need anything."

Rachel tried to dial Ella and nobody answered. I got my coat and Leah's and Leah got one of her animals and we put our sneakers on and Rachel still held the phone to her ear, waiting for somebody to answer. "I think we should go—let's just go," I said. But as soon as I got to the door and began to slide the chain along its track to unlock the door I felt uncertain. Maybe there was no fire, and the safest thing would be to stay inside. I slid the chain back into place.

"Ella's not answering," Rachel said. She joined us at the door, pulling on her jacket. "We should probably go down."

"Mommy and Daddy told us not to open the door," I said.

"Yeah, but if there's a fire and they're evacuating the building..."

"We don't know that. That's what he said, but maybe he wasn't really a fireman. It could be some bad man hiding around the corner waiting for us to open the door and then grab us."

Rachel reached for the chain. "That's ridiculous."

I grabbed Rachel's hand. "Rachel, don't. You don't know."

She shook my hand off of hers. "Let go of me. I think we should go."

"Then you should have answered the door," I screamed. "You were on the stupid phone and you didn't even come to the door when I said there was a fire."

Leah began to cry. "I want Mommy."

"Mommy's not here." I glared at her.

"So you think we should just stay here?" Rachel asked.

"I don't know what to do. But I don't think we should open the door."

Rachel peered through the peephole, then walked down the hallway to the living room and looked out the window.

"There's nothing to see out there," she said. "I don't care. We can do whatever you want." She pulled off her jacket and threw it onto a chair, stomped into her room and closed the door behind her.

"Wait, aren't you going to help me figure it out?" I called.

"I have homework."

"Homework? Homework? I hate her," I said to Leah.

"Are we going outside?"

"I don't know. I don't think so." I sat down on the black and white linoleum tiled floor right in front of the door. "You need a tissue."

Leah wiped her nose with her coat sleeve. "Can we finish our game?" she asked.

"No, I'm thinking."

"Can I take my coat off?"

"Yes."

She dropped her coat on the floor and went into our room. She returned with an armful of stuffed animals, dumped them on the floor, and went to retrieve another load. She arranged the animals in a circle on the floor, sat down, and started singing quietly: "Happy birthday to you, happy birthday to you..."

"What are you doing?" I asked.

"I'm having a birthday party for Tiger Stripe."

I watched her as she pretended that Tiger Stripe blew out the candles, and then she pretended to cut up the cake and distribute pieces to everybody. Was there a fire? Should we go? I could imagine unlocking the door, but I could not imagine pulling it open. Always there was a bad man waiting on the other side.

"Oh no," I said. "Oh no. Oh my god."

"What? What is it?"

"Look, there must be something wrong with the

birthday cake. All the animals are dying." I picked up one animal after another and made gruesome coughing sounds as each writhed on the floor. "This cake must be poisonous."

"It is not. They're not dying."

"I'm afraid they are. This birthday party has gone seriously amiss. We had better call the vet."

Leah looked around at the animals flung on the floor. "This is a terrible game. I don't like this game." She reached for Tiger Stripe and hugged her close.

I shook my head. "I guess the party's over. It's lucky for Rachel she wasn't here. She probably would have grabbed the first piece of cake. She would be dead now."

The doorbell rang.

"Girls—quick, open up, it's us." It was my mother's voice.

I released the chain and unlocked the door.

"Mommy," Leah fell into my mother's arms.

My mother looked around at the animals scattered on the floor. "Girls, there's a fire in the building, why are you still inside? Come, quick. Where's Rachel?"

As quiet as the back of our building had been, in front it was that noisy and busy and brightly lit. My parents led us over big burlap-covered hoses that extended all the way from the huge wheels on the fire engines down through the courtyard into the building, draping the street and the sidewalk. Men in yellow rubber coats and big black boots moved about, some with tanks on their backs, some carrying axes. They busied themselves with the hoses, or up on the trucks; the loud motor noise was punctuated with sharp static and voices coming through walkie-talkies. From inside our apartment I could never have imagined that this was taking place in front of our building.

My parents found a spot for us to stand a little bit apart from our neighbors, in the small, grassy triangular area across the street where people walked their dogs. I looked down as we walked, being careful not to step in dog poop. As my mother spoke to us, I watched a funnel of black smoke drift out of one of the windows, about halfway up the building.

"Why didn't you leave the apartment?" my mother said. She had to shout to be heard over all the noise. "We saw the fire engines and the flashing lights from all the way down the street—we didn't know which building it was until we got closer. You can imagine when I saw that smoke pouring out of our building... and then we looked all over for you, but we didn't see you anywhere. I was frantic. I asked a fireman—he said they knocked on all the doors. What were you thinking? Why didn't you come out?"

I began to cry.

"Well? Rachel?"

"Naomi thought we shouldn't open the door."

"Not open the door?" I could feel my mother's fury. "What were you thinking? That you knew better than the fireman? You could have been killed."

"Harriet..." said my father.

"You said we should never open the door. And Rachel was talking on the phone from the moment you left." I was screaming now. "You should be yelling at her, not at me. You shouldn't have left us. I didn't know. I thought..."

"Well, it's okay, we're all here now—we're safe," my

father said. But I did not feel safe. I looked at him. Where he was standing, the lights from the fire trucks made strange stripes over his face.

"Don't minimize it," my mother said sharply to my father. "What she did was very wrong. Very dangerous."

Rachel started to smile. "This is not a joke." My mother turned now to Rachel. "You should have known. Naomi's right. You were in charge. I should be able to leave you girls—"

"Look, there's Ella," said my father, waving his hand.

Ella made her way through the crowd to stand near us.

"You found them," said Ella. My mother reached across and tried to hug us all at the same time with an awkward embrace, pulling us into an uneven little circle. After an uncomfortable few seconds, she dropped her arms and turned to Ella.

"They were upstairs, can you imagine? This one thought it wasn't safe to leave the apartment." She motioned to me. I felt my face begin to flush. I didn't know if I would ever forgive my mother for saying that. Ella found my hand and squeezed it. What would it be like to have Ella for a mother?

The crowd of people pressed closer to us. There was a lot of loud talk. Some people were crying—the ones whose apartments were in the wing where the fire started—as they described all the furniture and books and clothes and paintings and papers and jewelry that they had had to leave behind in their apartments. Other people consoled themselves, saying: So long as no one is hurt. Thank god it didn't happen in the middle of the night. Can you imagine? We might have all been asleep. We could have died in our beds. Well, at least the firemen responded quickly. What if I hadn't been at home? Who would have known to rescue my parakeet?

And some just stood quietly, staring at the smoke.

I covered my nose and mouth with my hand and breathed in its smell—a faint remnant of the fried chicken we had had for dinner—in order to block out the smell of the smoke. Leah spotted an orange cat that someone had on a leash and went over to pet it. Rachel wrapped and unwrapped her jacket string around her fingers, over and over.

My mother asked Ella a lot of questions. "So now tell me, what happened, how did it happen, whose apartment?" It seemed to me that what she was asking was: whose fault was it? Like she wanted to find someone to blame.

Ella filled her in as much as she could. Apparently, nobody really knew what started the fire—there was no obvious cause. Many people thought it was an electrical fire that had started inside a wall. An electrical fire? I wondered about that—could a fire start just like that, inside a wall, because of the electrical wires? For no other reason? How could everything go along for years and years without a problem, and then all of a sudden there's a fire?

What was important to Ella, and what it took a while for my mother to finally understand, was that the fire began in an apartment on Ella's floor and that there was a good chance it might spread to her apartment. "Oh, Ella, what will you do? Let's just hope..." But I noticed something about my mother. It almost seemed like she was secretly happy when something bad happened to someone else and not to her.

The firemen were able to put out the fire before it spread to our side of the building. Later that night we returned to our apartments. We filed into the building and walked solemnly through the lobby—those of us who were allowed to. Ella's apartment had been flooded with water and she didn't yet know how much had been damaged. My mother invited her to stay overnight in our apartment but she went to her sister's instead.

As we crowded into the elevator with our neighbors I started thinking about the idea of an electrical fire. Could it be that those meters in the basement really were dangerous—that I had touched one and my touching it made something happen—set something in motion—that caused the fire? Had it been my fault? I didn't understand electrical fires, and I didn't understand how those electrical meters worked. And, anyway, I might not have touched one. And even if I did, those meters probably had nothing to do with this fire.

The elevator came to a halt at our floor. My family got out, but as we walked toward our apartment, I hung back behind my parents and my sisters. I didn't want to go in. I'm not sure why, but I was afraid that once we were all back in our apartment, with the door double-locked and the chain in place, the danger would be there, inside.

MISSING

It was recess and what I wanted was to be outside playing Bombardment, a game I loved and was especially good at. Instead, I sat on the toilet in a stall at my school bathroom, crying. On my lap I held a plastic bag containing a change of clothes—a bag that had sat unopened in my fifth-grade classroom cubby since the beginning of the school year. The clothes in there: a very ugly pair of denim dungarees, pinkish-red with the white warp thread showing through (not only very ugly but also too small, and the zipper didn't quite close right); a button-down man-tailored white shirt that had a brownish stain of unknown origin on the collar that I didn't remember having seen before (not just the stain but the shirt itself— probably it had been my older sister's); and an old pair of boy's sneakers, which were now too tight for me. I could not change into these clothes. I had tried them on in the stall, and even without looking in a mirror I could tell that I would never ever let anyone see me wearing them.

In other places they called it Dodgeball, but where I

went to school in NYC they called it Bombardment, and we also had another version we called Murder. In Bombardment there were two teams with a chalk line drawn between them on the asphalt playground, and we used not one but several of those red rubber bouncy balls that you'd throw at the opposing team in hopes of hitting someone, all the while trying to avoid getting hit yourself. If you were hit, you were out. But if you caught a ball that someone from the opposing team had thrown, they were out. Last week three of us—Daniel S., Daniel C., and me—began to keep track of how many times we could get someone out by catching the ball. So far, I was winning the contest. The Daniels were probably playing right now and adding more points to their totals. I wished I were outside playing. However, I couldn't play in the clothes I was wearing, a dress and patent leather Mary Janes, and I couldn't wear the clothes I would be able to play in, the horrible ones in the plastic bag on my lap. I would have to miss recess.

I never wore a dress to school. But today my mother made me wear a dress because it was Father's Day, the day when the school was only open half a day and fathers spent the half-day at school with their children. If it had been my father here with me I would have just worn my regular clothes, but he was away on business and so instead my grandfather was here, and because of that my mother had made me wear a dress. I not only had to wear a dress but was also supposed to be grateful and act friendly toward my grandfather for coming when really I wished he hadn't come at all. So now I sat, crying in the bathroom stall, and I wouldn't get to play during recess and my grandfather, anyway, had only been there with me a short time, because of course I had to share him with my sisters Rachel and Leah and my time with him was over and still I was stuck in this dress.

Before my father had left for France he had taken a few hours off from work one morning to go visit Leah's first-grade classroom. He had offered to spend some time with me in my class, too, but I had said no. The idea embarrassed me. It was one thing to have him there when all the other fathers were there, too, but on an ordinary school day? I couldn't imagine it. So he had gone only to Leah's class, and it turned out that he had made origami animals for them. I had never even known that he knew how to make any origami anything. Leah came home from school proudly carrying her origami elephant and said, "Look what Daddy made me, and he made them for the other kids, too." I stared at Leah and said, "He did? He did?" I didn't say to Leah, "He never made *me* an origami elephant." I didn't say anything to him when he came home that night after work.

And now he was in France. His company sent him there because he had been born in France and spoke French. I had no idea what he was doing there. Or what he did when he went to work at home. He was in textiles: that's all I knew.

I got up from the toilet and went over to the sink to look in the mirror. Who was that girl in the ridiculous plaid dress with the white Peter Pan collar? It couldn't possibly be me. No, this was not Naomi.

My eyes were red from crying. I splashed water on my face and then kept splashing and splashing. I had put the plastic bag down on the edge of the sink basin, and now the clothes in the bag were getting all wet and I didn't care.

I didn't care if they got all moldy sitting in the plastic bag: I knew I was never ever going to wear those clothes. And if they began to smell and the whole classroom started to smell I didn't care either. Father's Day was a stupid thing anyway.

That night Leah suggested that we have a birthday party with our stuffed animals. Leah often liked to have cake and ice cream with her animals but was especially excited about it in anticipation of my tenth birthday party, which was coming up on Saturday. I was sitting comfortably on her bed and in the middle of a good book— *Knight's Castle* by Edward Eager. I had no desire to stop reading, but I often had a hard time saying no to Leah.

"Let's play a game first before we eat the birthday cake," said Leah. "What game should we play?"

"Why don't we have a staring contest?" I suggested.

Leah didn't know what a staring contest was. I explained it to her. We set all the animals up in pairs on the rug. I paired myself with Tiger Stripe, the largest of the animals, and Leah with Little Lamb, who looked shyly up at Leah with her head tilted, but then she always had that look, ever since our grandmother had washed her in the washing machine and most of her neck stuffing had come out.

"Okay, now when I say go, the contest begins," I explained. "Remember, whoever looks away first or smiles or laughs, loses. Is everybody ready?"

"Ready," said Leah.

"One, two, three, go."

Of course it was impossible to beat a stuffed animal in a staring contest. I propped my book up against Tiger

Stripe's body and continued to read. From time to time I called out, "Everyone still going?"

Leah stared very intently at the stuffed animal's face, her own head cocked in a mirror image of Little Lamb's. "Are you allowed to talk?" asked Leah.

"You can talk but you can't look away or smile."

After a while Leah asked, "How will we know when this is over?"

"When someone in each pair wins." I began to feel a little guilty. "Or when I call out that time is up." I read to the end of a chapter, and then reluctantly closed my book. "Okay, time is up. Good job everybody. You all win."

It was time for cake, but just then our mother came in to say that it was time for Leah to brush her teeth and get ready for bed.

"But we didn't have the cake yet," Leah protested.

"Cake will have to wait until tomorrow," our mother said.

"That was a terrible game, that staring game," Leah said to me. "It took so long, now we can't have cake."

"Sorry," I said. "Next time you choose the game." I returned to my book.

In the mornings I missed my father the most. It wasn't that I missed him exactly, that wasn't the right word. But overnight I forgot that he was away. I would open my eyes expecting to see him, since it was always my father who came in to wake us up on school days, standing by each of our beds in turn, grinning as he sang: "*Chère Nomi, Chère Leah, dormez-vous, dormez vous?*" But instead of my father, it was my mother, calling out from the doorway. "Girls—Leah, Naomi—it's time to get up." Then I would remember: oh yeah, Daddy's not here.

At recess the next day, Daniel S. told me that he and Daniel C. had decided they wouldn't count yesterday's Bombardment game since I hadn't been able to play. I felt happy. I was in my clothes, my usual clothes, my favorite pair of dungarees and my sneakers, and a very soft blue and white striped T-shirt. I felt so good in those clothes! And I knew I could beat both Daniels in this contest. We decided to keep track for another week.

I couldn't explain it. I was good at Bombardment and I had always been very good at catching the balls, but there was something about turning it into a contest that made me play even better. I somehow knew I would win. That day I made twenty-five catches, the most ever. Every time someone threw a ball at me I just reached out my arms and let the ball sink into my body as I grabbed onto it and held it tight. The Daniels didn't even come close.

I thought Daniel S. might like me a little bit. A few weeks earlier he had started giving me the lead from his pencils. I wasn't sure why, or what to do with it, but he had gotten in the habit of breaking open his pencils and removing the lead. His aim was to keep the lead intact as he broke the pencil open. Apparently, this was hard to do. I didn't understand it, but I saved the lead he gave me in the little gutter in my desk. It was getting awkward because he kept giving me more and more and I was running out of room. I didn't know what to do with all the lead. If I put it inside my desk where I kept my books and papers it would get everything all dirty. I didn't really want the lead, but I didn't want to say anything that would make him stop giving it to me, because it made me feel good that he did that.

The next morning I lay in bed, not really wanting to get up to go to school, thinking about my father, and about my mother, and about how differently they each greeted me in the morning. I wondered, am I like my father? Did he ever think, "Naomi is my daughter and she reminds me of myself when I was her age?" I was always looking for ways in which we were alike, but I wasn't ever sure it mattered to my father. Did he want me to be like him? Did he even think about it at all? My mother on the other hand would frequently go on and on about how she and I were both middle children, the middle one of three girls, and because of that she claimed to understand me very well. I didn't feel that my mother understood me at all. Her situation had been entirely different from mine. *Her* older sister enjoyed doing things with her, as if they were friends. *My* older sister wanted nothing to do with me. My mother assumed I was just like her. I knew I wasn't.

Now I could hear my mother yelling at me and at Leah, who also hadn't gotten out of bed yet, that we were going to be late for school if we didn't get out of bed that minute. I didn't feel like moving. Where was my father now? Was he thinking about me? Did he miss me at all? Did he tell the people he met about me? I wondered what he would say if he told anybody about me. Would it be something special about me? Or would it just be, I have three daughters. I pictured him in a toy store, picking out three dolls for his daughters, and telling the shop clerk, "These dolls are for my three daughters." He never seemed to understand that I didn't play with dolls. I began to feel a little angry with him. Then I heard my mother rummaging around in the hall closet, and all of a sudden I was assaulted by the extremely loud roar of the vacuum cleaner. I couldn't bear it. All I wanted was to lie in my bed in quiet. Leah made her way out of bed and went over to our mother, who was vacuuming right outside their door.

"What are you doing?" Leah shouted over the sound of the vacuum cleaner.

"You girls wouldn't get out of bed. I thought this would do the trick."

I tried to block the sound out by covering my ears with my pillow but it didn't work. I got up out of bed and screamed, "Okay, okay, turn it off already, we're awake." I was in a bad mood all day.

That day at recess a lot of the kids decided to play Spin the Bottle instead of Bombardment. Daniel S. said to me, "Are you going to play Spin the Bottle?"

"What about our Bombardment contest?" I asked.

"I would rather play Spin the Bottle," Daniel shrugged.

I didn't know what to say. Maybe he didn't like it that he was losing. For me it wasn't so much about the contest, it was just that I really enjoyed playing Bombardment. I had no interest in kissing games. And now I worried that Daniel S. would stop giving me the lead from his pencils.

The two Daniels both decided to play Spin the Bottle, along with a number of other kids. There really weren't enough left to play Bombardment, so I wandered aimlessly over to sit down on a swing, twisting one way and then the other while keeping my feet on the ground. I could see the group playing Spin the Bottle on the far side of the playground. I noticed the occasional glint of the green bottle in someone's hand, then two kids at a time would stand up and step away from the circle and lean their faces toward each other. I didn't understand the point of it. I couldn't see well, but I could tell when it was Daniel S. who stood because he was the shortest boy in the class and much shorter than any of the girls, so when it was his turn to kiss he had to stand on tip-toes and crane his neck to reach the girl while she bent down to him. It seemed like such a stupid game. But I continued to watch.

I wondered whether anyone ever looked at me without my knowing. And if they did, what did they think about me? Sometimes when we drove somewhere, like to visit my grandparents in Brooklyn, I pretended I was asleep in the back seat of the car at the end of the ride home. I liked hearing my parents talk about me, even if mostly all they said was, "Is she asleep?" "Yes, she's asleep." The sound of their voices talking about me sent little tingles down my spine. I always hoped they would say something more, really notice me and comment on how I looked and say something nice about me. But invariably they just woke me up.

At dinner that night my mother talked about the doll she had bought for Rachel when I was born. For some reason, every year around the time of my birthday my mother loved to tell this story. It was an enormous doll, bigger than me, and Rachel had lost it almost immediately. My mother left me at home with my grandmother and took Rachel to the supermarket. When they got to the checkout counter my mother noticed that the doll was missing. She asked Rachel where it was, and Rachel didn't know, so they retraced their steps up and down the aisles, but they couldn't find the doll. I didn't have any idea why my mother always told this story. I pictured the doll with frozen features painted on its big plastic head, peering out from behind stacks of cereal boxes or spaghetti, watching my mother and Rachel walk by, wanting to shout out, "Here I am, here I am, I'm right here." But it couldn't speak.

After dinner, while Rachel was taking a shower, I went into her room. For some reason I had an urge to look at the display case of dolls that my father had brought back from the various countries he traveled to on business. Each one was dressed in an elaborate costume from her native country. I never knew what to say to my father when he gave me a doll. Dolls! Who did he think I was? I never played with dolls. And these were not even meant for playing with. Did he think I cared about their costumes? Fancy dresses? Rachel and Leah were always excited in anticipation of getting another doll, but I thought the dolls were just dumb and had nothing to do with me. Why didn't he know that? I was working myself up into a good fury. "I hate these stupid dolls," I said in a tight voice. "Why do you keep getting us these stupid dolls?"

The party was going to be on Saturday afternoon, and we were going to play games and then eat fried chicken and birthday cake and then I would open my presents. In the morning when I woke up, my room smelled of fried chicken: my mother had already started cooking. Leah was lying in her bed having conversations with her animals, but when I woke up, Leah climbed into my bed. We lay in bed holding hands, not saying anything. I stared up at the ceiling, then looked around the room. I was happy just lying there smelling the fried chicken smell, and I felt excited that this was the day of my party. This had been Leah's room before I moved in. The wallpaper had a repeating pattern of different zoo animals. I had never thought much about it before, but today I thought, this is Leah's wallpaper. I wondered whether there was anything in this room, or anyplace in the whole apartment, that you could tell belonged to me. Not my books or my clothes or something like that which could be moved, but something more permanent, like the wallpaper. What would it be? Was there something that people associated immediately with me, that you knew, oh yes, that must be Naomi's place? The way my mother's toilet water left that smell behind in her closet and on all her clothes. Did I have anything like that at all? Leah, of course, had animals: it was easy to get Leah birthday presents because you knew she would like all animals or anything to do with animals. But I didn't know what people thought about me when they thought about getting something that I would like. There were things I might like that anybody would like. But was there anything that was just exactly the thing that I would like? As I lay in bed thinking these thoughts, I began to feel nervous about my party.

At the party, everyone but me was crowded into the bathroom because we were ducking for apples in the bathtub. I had thought it would be a fun thing to do when my mother suggested it, but now, standing outside the bathroom, I wasn't sure. The way we were doing it, everyone was divided into two teams and one person from each team took a turn at the same time, both trying to be the first to get an apple in her mouth. It was crowded in the bathroom and it was messy and I wondered, was it unsanitary? Other people didn't seem to worry about that kind of thing, but I did. One time my mother had said to me: you're eating so much, maybe you have a tapeworm. I hadn't known what a tapeworm was. My mother told me it was a worm that lived inside your stomach and ate everything you swallowed, so you always felt hungry. I got really worried—I pictured a huge worm that was nestled in my intestines, the entire length of the intestines, which I knew when extended were very very long, and whenever I ate something it was there with its mouth open just waiting for the food. After that, whenever I felt particularly hungry I wondered: do I have a tapeworm in me? Thinking about tapeworms gave me the thought that maybe there was a worm in one of those apples. Usually I looked very carefully before taking a bite from an apple because I knew that worms hid in apples. I began to worry that when it was my turn to dunk, I might bite into an apple and accidentally swallow a worm. So I stood just outside the bathroom door—there really wasn't room for everyone in the bathroom—and I couldn't help thinking about the possibility of swallowing a worm, which gave me a nervous feeling in my stomach. Just then the phone began to ring and as the phone rang and rang, my mother, who had been in the bathroom supervising the apple-ducking, made her way out through the crowd of kids. She held a towel and was drying her hands with a very triumphant look on her face that I didn't know how to interpret. The phone continued to ring as my mother rushed to the kitchen. Then it stopped and my mother shouted out, "Naomi, it's for you." I thought it must be my grandparents calling to wish me a happy birthday. I went into the kitchen and my mother handed me the phone with a big smile. I held it up to my ear and said a tentative "Hello?"

"Happy Birthday Naomi!" It was my father. I felt my face flush. This was completely unexpected. I didn't know you could call from France to New York. I thought I just had to get used to him being gone, and after a while I didn't think I missed him. I wasn't even sure I liked him—thinking about him being away on my birthday, and the origami he made for Leah but not for me, and all those stupid dolls he brought home for us, and did he even think about me? But hearing his voice... I felt overwhelmed with feelings for him, good feelings of loving him, and sad feelings because he was so far away and he wasn't here with me.

My mother stood beaming and gesturing at me to say something. All I could do was hold onto the phone while saying nothing. "Are you having fun at your party?" my father asked. There was too much feeling and I couldn't find any words.

On Monday morning when I arrived at school, I saw that someone had put a present in my cubby. There it sat— wrapped in shiny gold paper—a cube about ten inches on each side, with a card scotch-taped to the top. I removed the card and read:

"This is for you, Naomi, because you won the Bombardment contest. From, Daniel S. and Daniel P."

I turned around and saw the Daniels looking at me, grinning. They walked over to where I stood by my cubby. "Should I open it?" I asked, uncertain. They nodded. I tore off the wrapping paper to reveal a cardboard box containing a brand-new red rubber Bombardment ball. I thought it was the best present I had ever received.

We were getting ready to leave for the airport to go pick up my father. I looked at myself in the mirror. I worried about my bangs; I had started to grow them out. Actually, it was my mother's idea—both Leah and I were growing out our bangs—but it meant that they had to be held to the side with barrettes until they actually grew long enough to be incorporated into braids or a ponytail. I suddenly feared that the barrettes looked really stupid or ugly, or really childish—that they were okay for Leah but not for me. I looked at them in the mirror for a long time, unsure, until Rachel said to me, "It's only Daddy." I blushed a little. "There's something in my eye, stupid." I leaned closer to the mirror.

On the way to the airport, Rachel and Leah both sat in the front with our mother while I sat quietly alone in the back seat and stared out the window.

The darkness was punctuated by passing headlights and streetlamps and indeterminate shapes of cars and buildings. As I stared, I noticed that my eyes automatically and continuously shifted from left to right to track the motion of the objects outside the window. It was impossible to stare out of a moving car and keep your eyes from moving. I had never noticed that before. But was it really impossible? I tried to hold my eyes in a fixed position but it was not easy. Soon they started to hurt, so I gave up. Gradually the motion of the car, the murmur of voices coming from the front seat, and the flicker of lights and shapes outside lulled me to sleep. I awoke to see

Rachel peering over the front seat, saying, "She's not really asleep, she always fakes it." We were parked in the lot across from the International Arrivals Building.

The second floor of the building had a balcony with glass walls through which you could look down and see the arriving travelers pass through Customs. I stood with my mother and my sisters, all four of us staring at the commotion down below, hoping to spot my father. Leah had the binoculars and kept shouting, "I see him, I see him," but she was always mistaken.

At a certain point I noticed that I could use the glass wall as a mirror. If I caught the light at just the right angle, I could see myself very faintly in the glass. At the same time, through the reflection of my own face, I could also see the people milling about down below, many pushing carts filled with their belongings. Just as I realized this, I saw someone who looked a lot like my father pushing his cart right about where my cheekbone was, and as he kept walking and walked right into my eye, I felt sure it was him and I almost called out, "That's him, I see him," but just then he stopped and stood right in my pupil. Instead of saying anything, I concentrated on moving my head slightly so that he was now standing on my forehead. Then I moved my head again and he was on my cheek, then my mouth, then back in my eye.

Leah shouted out once more, "I see him, I see him." She began to bang on the window to catch his attention.

I remained frozen for one more second, then reached out to take the binoculars from Leah.

"Leah, stop that now, he can't hear you," said our mother.

"But he's right there." Leah pointed with her finger on

the glass.

I watched through the binoculars as he pushed his cart forward. Soon he was next in line to have his luggage searched. He bent down to start unloading the contents of a couple of shopping bags. The person ahead of him was finished and the Customs official motioned to my father to open his suitcases. I could see the two of them talking and pointing.

Finally my father was waved through. He closed up his suitcases and as he was repacking the shopping bags my mother said, "Daddy's made it through customs. Come, let's go down and meet him." She started walking toward the elevators with Rachel and Leah close behind. But I continued to watch him through the binoculars. I saw him place a doll wearing a fancy dress at the top of one of the shopping bags. Then, as he began to wheel his cart through the doorway, I watched the doll topple off the bag, falling onto the floor. My father didn't seem to have noticed.

Leah, meanwhile, noticed that I was not with them; she stopped to turn around and yelled out to me, "Come on, Naomi. You'll miss the elevator."

My father and his cart disappeared through the door.

"Come on, come on," Leah insisted.

But still I didn't move. I couldn't move. I was transfixed watching the scene unfold below through the binoculars. The doll lay on the floor. The next person, a woman in high heels wearing a black coat with a fur collar, wheeled her cart toward the doors. When she reached the doll, the front right wheel bumped up against it and the cart came to a full stop.

I knew right away that what I wanted was for the

woman to roll her cart right over that doll. I wanted the doll to be entirely crushed. I wondered: Is it possible you can make something happen just by staring at it? If you imagine something and you hope it will happen, even if you're not sure why you hope it, then just by looking and concentrating hard can you make it happen?

The woman pulled the cart back a little and then pushed. Again the cart ran into the doll and was prevented from moving forward. After pausing a moment, she pulled the cart back several feet and then leaned into the cart using her whole body to push it forward. This time the wheel finally made it over the doll, crushing it.

I lowered the binoculars and headed toward the elevator. I felt very satisfied. It was as though it had actually been me, Naomi, who had pushed that cart myself and had used my own strength to run right over that doll. What would my father say when he discovered that the doll was missing? And what would I say? Would I tell him what I had seen? I wasn't entirely sure, but I thought I would say nothing.

THE EXPLORER PROJECT

This is how Dana and I became friends:

In sixth grade our teacher, Miss Sanders, alerted our class that we were going to have an assignment about explorers. We would have to do some research and write something and draw a map. She would assign us an explorer and a partner to work with. What I wanted was a partner who was a friend and an explorer who didn't travel too far and who didn't make a lot of trips. Maybe he had died in the middle of the first one. I was not good at drawing. I figured half a trip would be as much of a drawing as I could handle.

Miss Sanders looked at me. "Naomi, you'll be paired with Dana and you will have Ferdinand Magellan." Magellan! He traveled around the whole world! And Dana. This was a bad draw on both counts. I looked over at Dana. She was looking the other way. I couldn't tell how she felt about it. She was twirling a strand of hair and absent-mindedly put the end of it in her mouth. When she turned and saw me watching her, a slow blush crept up on her cheek. But she did not look away. And she did not remove the hair from her mouth.

When I started at this school in fourth grade, Dana was not there, but everybody talked about her all the time. From what they said it seemed to me that everyone admired her greatly and waited for her opinion before forming their own. I decided I didn't like this Dana. Even though she wasn't there, everyone still wondered what she would think about things. Who is this Dana? I thought. Who does she think she is?

My second year at the school—fifth grade—Dana was back. Because she had been in England the previous year she spoke with an accent. I noticed that after a few weeks the accent faded. She seemed to have lost her authority in the year she was away, but I still felt a little wary of her. We didn't become friends.

Now we were going to have to meet after school to work on the project. We each lived about half a mile from the school, in opposite directions. In order to be fair, we decided to meet twice, once at her house, once at my apartment.

When Dana came to my apartment she stood in the doorway of my room and looked all around. Nobody had ever looked at my room so closely. She asked a lot of questions.

"Wow, are all those stuffed animals yours?"

"No, that's Leah's bed. Those are all hers."

"Did you choose this wallpaper?" she asked.

"No, this was Leah's room before we shared it. It's her wallpaper." I would never have chosen this wallpaper: baby zoo animals in yellows and oranges.

"Why did you move in with Leah?"

"I was sharing a room with Rachel but she wasn't nice to me. Really what I wanted was my own room."

"So why couldn't you have it? Why couldn't Rachel and Leah share a room?"

"Because they're too far apart in age."

Dana looked skeptical. "Did you want to change the wallpaper?"

I shook my head. I had never thought about changing the wallpaper. Maybe I should have.

"Do you both go to bed at the same time?"

"No, of course not. Leah is younger than me."

"So what do you do if you want to be in your room after she goes to sleep? Can you be in here with a light on?"

"I can read in bed with a flashlight."

"What if you don't want to read in bed?"

"I go somewhere else. I sit in the living room." Dana was making me uncomfortable with her questions. I really had wanted my own room, but that wasn't a possibility. And it was much much better to share a room with Leah than with Rachel, who used to kick me out of the room and close the door, even though it was my room, too. With Leah it was the opposite: she always wanted me to play with her, even when I wanted to be doing something else. But at least she was friendly.

Dana stared at my desk. There wasn't much to look at, just stuff from school piled up on one side.

"You don't have any pictures on your desk. Or any pictures or anything up on the walls. It's like the room is Leah's room and you're just a visitor staying in it."

I shrugged. For some reason, even though it made me uncomfortable, I began to like the attention Dana was paying to me and to my room. I could understand a little bit why other kids had deferred to her. Like she understood something I had sensed but hadn't exactly been able to articulate before. We went into the living room to get the World Book Encyclopedia, and we looked up Magellan.

Dana lived in a house. She had her own room and it was very different from mine. It was painted a pale blue and there were pictures on the wall of the kings and queens of England and a picture of London and a poster of the Beatles and one that said, "War is not healthy for children and other living things," and also lots of small photographs of different people. It was as though you could know Dana from looking at her room whereas in my room you had to wonder, who was Naomi?

Neither of us was excited about Magellan. He had traveled all around the whole entire world and a lot of people died. And he also made a bunch of other voyages before that, which meant more drawing. Dana was not very good at drawing, either. She suggested that before actually sitting down to do anything, we should make a plan, talk about it, and that her favorite place for talking was in the enclosed porch where the ping-pong table was. We could hit the ball back and forth and talk. Did I like ping-pong? Did I want to do that?

I liked ping-pong quite a lot. I had played at camp the summer before. At first, I only knew how to hit the ball with a backhand, but one of the other campers taught me to do a forehand, and then she taught me how to put spin on the ball and even how to slam the ball. The slam was really fun, even when the ball missed the table. Whenever

I had the chance, I tried for a slam. By the end of camp, I was beating her frequently. That really annoyed her.

We went out on the porch and started hitting the ball gently back and forth. We didn't begin to talk right away. We were busy concentrating on getting a rhythm with the ping-pong ball. Then Dana spoke. "Okay, what are we going to do about this map of Magellan?"

"Magellan, why did she have to give us stupid Magellan?"

"What do you think about Miss Sanders?"

"She's kind of strict." That's what everyone said about her. I wasn't really sure what I thought about her, except that she made me feel shy.

"Yes, she's strict, but do you think it's a good strict or a bad strict?"

"I don't know."

"I like her. I think she's a good strict."

I wasn't really sure what Dana was talking about, which was the same feeling I often had around Miss Sanders.

"What's a good strict?"

"She's strict because she knows what she thinks you should be doing. Unlike Mrs. Feldstein." Mrs. Feldstein had been our fifth-grade teacher the year before. She was no longer at our school because she was going to have a baby.

"Mrs. Feldstein wasn't strict at all."

"Yes, and she was a very bad teacher." Dana was so definite. "I'm going to be a teacher so I pay a lot of attention to my teachers. I have a notebook where I write down what I think about stuff they do or say. The good things and the bad things. That way when I'm older and a teacher myself I will remember how it felt."

"You keep a notebook?" None of my friends ever did anything like that.

"Yeah. And Mrs. Feldstein did or said a lot of bad things. What did you think about her?" asked Dana.

"I don't know."

"It sure seemed like you didn't like her. You used to argue with her all the time."

This was true. Something had happened to me last year with Mrs. Feldstein. It started with an argument one time during a spelling bee, about how she had pronounced a word. I was the best speller in our class. I don't mean to brag but it was just a fact. Whenever we had a spelling bee Mrs. Feldstein would make two teams and we would line up one by one on either side of the classroom as she called out our names and directed us to one side or the other. She always saved me for last and she would ask the whole class, "Which team should I put Naomi on?" There I was, the only one left sitting at my desk in the middle of the room, and everybody would be shouting out, "Our team! Our side!" because they knew, it was just true, that whatever team I was on would win since I always spelled all the words correctly. Mrs. Feldstein would give us each a word, one by one, and gradually there would be fewer and fewer standing on each side because you had to go back to your desk if you made a mistake. It always came down to two kids—me on one side and someone on the other side—and then I always spelled every word right, and the other kid eventually spelled something wrong. I would be the last one standing, and my team would win.

On that day of my first argument with her, we were having a spelling bee, and I misspelled a word, which I'd never done before. The word was "anticlimactic" and I missed the second "c." I told her it was because she pronounced it wrong. I said that if she had said it right I would have spelled it right, so I should get a new word. She pronounced it "anti-climatic," but I told her she should have said "anti-climactic." I convinced her. It was satisfying to argue and win and after that, I started to argue with her about other things. Not meanly, or by yelling at her, but just through using logic. It felt really good.

"Do you know that she lives in the apartment building next to mine?" I said.

Dana was very interested. "You know where she lives?"

"Yeah, right next door."

"Can we get inside the building?"

"Probably."

"Maybe we could write her a letter about how bad a teacher she was and slip it under her door."

"You would really do that? Isn't that kind of mean?"

"I think a teacher should be told if they did something bad. Because they have a big effect on their students."

"Did she do something bad to you? That had a bad effect?"

"She could have taught me how to be a better speller, but instead she always had those stupid spelling bees. Everybody knew that you were the best speller and that Daniel S. was the worst, but if he ever spelled something right she said something nice about how we should all congratulate him because his spelling was improving. The rest of us got no help from her. We just had to go through that same thing, week after week: wait for your turn and spell the word in front of everybody. If you did it right she didn't say anything nice, she just went on to the next kid with the next word and if you did it wrong the other team cheered and your own team glared at you while you made your way back to your desk. What a stupid waste of time."

"I never thought about those spelling bees like that."

"Well of course: you always were the last one standing. It might not have been bad for you, but think about everyone else."

I guess she had a point.

"And another thing, she could have realized that you and I could be friends. She could have done something to make that happen. Like Miss Sanders made us partners because she knew we should be friends and we needed something to help us get started. And so now we're friends. But Mrs. Feldstein—the whole year in her class and she didn't do anything to make it happen."

Were we friends now? I had never known any other kid who thought about things in this way. Or if they did think about these things, they never talked about them with me. With my other friends we just played games or baked cookies or went ice-skating or stuff like that. Played ping-pong but didn't use ping-pong for talking. Did Miss Sanders think we should be friends? Did teachers actually care about that?

"Don't you agree we should write the letter? Not just for us, but for all the students that she didn't help? And if she ever goes back to teaching again?"

"I guess we could do it if sometime you came over to my apartment again. When we're done with this project." If Dana came to my apartment not just to work on a school project that would make us friends. Actually, I was kind of hoping that if we waited, Dana would forget about the whole thing, because thinking about writing a mean letter to Mrs. Feldstein and slipping it under her door gave me a nervous feeling in my stomach.

The next few weeks we met at Dana's house and read more about Magellan. Everywhere it said that Magellan was the first to sail around the world but then the more you read the more you found out that he had died before they even made it to Africa. Actually, it was Juan Sebastian Elcano who finished the trip. And even though it wasn't Magellan at the end, we still had to draw the whole route. As we drew, we spent a lot of time talking about the other kids in our class, and my mind thought of things to say that I didn't know were inside me—observations and explanations and questions. This was a different kind of friendship than I had ever had.

And then we finished the explorer project and Dana came over to my apartment to write the letter to Mrs. Feldstein.

She sat on my bed with her notebook open on her lap. "Dear Mrs. Feldstein, We're writing to tell you what a bad teacher you are. We barely learned anything at all last year. We don't think you are very smart."

"What else should we say?" asked Dana.

I was feeling uneasy. Had she truly been such a bad teacher? She had always tried so hard to get us to like her— maybe that was her problem. This letter was going to really hurt her feelings, after all that effort.

"Are you sure we should do this?"

Dana looked at me coldly. "I thought you wanted to do this. You agreed she was a bad teacher."

"I guess so."

Dana started writing again in her notebook. "If you hadn't quit you would have been fired. We feel sorry for your baby to have a mother like you."

That seemed really mean to me, but Dana was laughing.

"Okay, that's enough," Dana said, offering me the notebook. "Why don't you sign your name?"

"Wait, we're signing our names to this? Then she'll know who wrote it."

"Well, duh."

Until now it had seemed almost like some kind of joke. Maybe a mean joke, but not very risky.

"But I don't really—I mean, I didn't think we would... I just thought..."

"Okay, we don't have to sign it, if you're really too scared. Do you have an envelope we can put it in?"

"I think my Mom has one somewhere. I'll go check."

When I came back to the room Dana had already removed the paper from the notebook and folded it. I handed her the envelope. She put the paper in, licked the flap, and sealed it shut with a certain kind of authority. "So how do we get there?"

It was a pretty cold, raw November day and getting dark already. We walked outside and I led Dana down the street and around the corner.

"Hey, I thought you said she lived right next door."

"She lives right next door on the back side of my building. Don't worry. I'm taking us there." My apartment building was much bigger than any of the others near it. It extended between two streets, whereas Mrs. Feldstein's building and all the others were less than half as deep. I had taken us out the front of my building because the only way out the back was through the basement, and the basement scared me. I tried to avoid it whenever I could.

"It's cold out. Why didn't we go out the back?"

"Just follow me." I led her into the entryway of Mrs. Feldstein's building. Hanging on the wall beside the big double glass door into the lobby was an intercom with a directory of names and apartments. Dana pushed and pulled at the doors, but they were locked.

"How are we supposed to get in?"

"No problem," I said. Dana was not used to the ways of apartment buildings, but I was. I stood staring at the directory.

"Got it," I said, and pointed to the name—Feldstein, apartment 3-J.

"You're not going to push her buzzer, are you?"

"Don't worry." I liked being the expert. Of course I wasn't going to push her buzzer. The point was to slip the note under her door and get out of there as fast as possible before she could see us. Instead I pushed a couple of buttons on the sixth, the highest floor. A voice came through the intercom: "Who is it?" I didn't answer. I pushed a couple more buttons. Someone buzzed the door open, and we walked into the lobby.

"People just let you in without knowing who it is? Won't they be expecting someone to appear at their apartment?"

"Sometimes it's too much trouble to ask who it is. If nobody shows up, they figure it was a delivery person who pushed the wrong button." The elevator was right in front of us, but I was looking around for the staircase. We didn't want to have to rely on the elevator on the way down. I felt oddly powerful, knowing my way around so well, figuring out all the angles.

"What are you doing now?" asked Dana.

I found the door to the stairs.

"Follow me," I said.

We climbed up to the third floor and opened the door to the hallway, a long corridor with doors on either side. I put my finger to my lips, and walked quietly, looking for apartment 3-J. It was all the way down at the end, furthest from the stairs. Dana stopped in front of her door, but I turned around and kept walking, back to the stairwell. She looked puzzled but followed after me. When we got to the stairwell she asked, "What's the matter?"

"We need to make a plan. We didn't even decide who would be the one to slip the letter under her door. One of us should wait here, I think. Then whoever puts it under the door can just run quickly and we can get away fast."

"I think you're making too big a deal of this. We're just slipping it under her door. Who even knows if she's there?" Dana had the letter in her hand, and she started walking back down the hallway to Mrs. Feldstein's door. I had that nervous feeling in my stomach. I wasn't sure whether to wait in the stairwell or not. Dana seemed completely unafraid. I took a few steps and hovered there while Dana slipped the letter under the door. I expected her to run away but she didn't: she stood there calmly, almost as though she wanted Mrs. Feldstein to open the door and find her. I was getting more and more nervous. Then Dana turned around to walk back toward me, but before she actually started walking she turned once again, reached up to the doorbell, and pushed it. Laughing and screaming, she raced down the hallway and grabbed me, pulled me into the stairwell and down the stairs. We ran down the stairs as fast as we could and then outside.

Dana began to walk toward the back of my building.

"It's freezing out here," she said. "Let's go in this way."

I could not tell her that I tried never to go into the basement. One time when I was quite young, maybe five years old, I had been with a friend of mine, Susie, who also lived in the building. We followed her mother through the basement and as we were walking up the ramp out to the street I punched her in the face. Her nose began to bleed. She was upset and crying and I started to cry. Her mother turned around, and through her tears Susie said, "Naomi hit me." I was crying even harder than she was and her mother asked me, "Naomi, why did you hit Susie?" who by now had stopped crying and was no longer bleeding. I was still crying very hard and I didn't know why I had hit Susie. I had never done that before. I thought that somehow it had to do with the basement.

I didn't want to be interrogated by Dana. She seemed unable to understand fear. I led her down the path that led to the ramp to the basement. The basement doors were big old heavy rusty metal doors that often were hard to open.

"Boy," she said after I had been struggling for a while with the door. "They don't make it easy."

Finally, the door opened and we entered the basement. It was dark and our eyes had to adjust before we could see anything. The floors were concrete, dirty, stained in places, and the basement smelled of mildew. It was enormous and we could not see all the way in.

"Wow, what a weird place." Dana walked over to the wall where there were rows of electrical meters, row upon row of glass-encased dials, more than one hundred of them, one for every apartment in the building. She reached out her hand.

"Don't!" I shouted. "Don't touch them."

Dana laughed. "Why not?"

"You could get electrocuted." My mother had always told me never ever to touch the meters. One time I almost thought I had touched one by accident, and nothing happened, but I was never sure. Better to be safe.

"That's ridiculous," said Dana. "We have these at my house. Not so many, of course." She reached out her hand and touched one of the glass enclosures with her finger. "It's just a piece of glass." I waited for her to sizzle and fall to the floor in convulsions. She did neither. She laughed.

"Can we look around some?" She started to walk toward the back part of the basement where the storage lockers were.

"The elevator is this way," I said, pointing in the other direction. I was ready for Dana to go home. I had no desire to walk back there with her. It was too spooky.

"Can't I look around a little? This is really cool."

It was not cool. It was dark and dirty and smelly and felt dangerous. I wanted to get to the elevators and go upstairs as quickly as possible but I wasn't sure that I should leave her to wander around by herself.

"I'm going up," I said.

Dana walked back toward me and then veered off down another dark corridor.

"What's down here?"

"There's another elevator. Not for my section of the building. That way is the furnace and over there are the storage lockers. And there are two other elevators also. It's really not that interesting."

"The furnace?"

"Yeah, for the garbage. You know how we throw our garbage down that little chute? It all lands down here and then they burn it."

"Wow, everybody's garbage all in one big pile? Can we watch it?"

I didn't understand why Dana was so interested. "No, it's really not safe."

"Can we look in the storage lockers?"

"It's mostly a lot of junk. And, anyway, most of them are locked. Come on, let's go."

I walked toward the elevator and pressed the button. Dana followed me.

"We'll definitely have to come down here again."

Suddenly I just felt sad. I was tired of Dana. I couldn't help imagining Mrs. Feldstein opening that envelope and reading the letter and feeling very hurt. Why had I done it? I got swept up in it and now I wished I hadn't. Dana was so sure that she knew what made a good teacher and a bad teacher, but what about a good person? What we had done was really not nice.

The elevator was taking a long time to get there. You always had to wait much longer in the basement. We stood and stared at the closed elevator door. Then Dana pushed the button.

"It doesn't help to push it again," I said. "We just have to wait."

"I signed our names on the letter," Dana said.

"What? You did what?"

"I signed our names," said Dana with a grin.

"How could you do that? We decided we wouldn't. You said we wouldn't."

"I changed my mind."

"And you signed my name when I said I didn't want to? But now she'll know it was me. What if I see her?" I began to cry.

I wanted to undo it and there was no way to make it not have happened. Not to have done it. The whole thing was a mistake and I couldn't change it. I had ventured into this friendship with Dana and it turned out to be very dangerous and even if I found my way out, still there would be this thing I had done that I could not erase.

"What's wrong with this elevator?" Dana said. "I'm going to look around. Are you gonna come with me?" She began to walk away.

Magellan's crew did mutiny at one point. It was when they couldn't find the way around South America. They wanted to turn around and go back to Spain. But he took care of that—he killed one of the two mutinous captains and left the other behind on some island. Then they all had to keep going. They must have felt terrible and wished they hadn't gone along with him in the first place. And in the end, out of five ships and 270 crewmembers, only one ship and 18 people made it all the way. Everybody else died. Including Magellan. And did he ever feel bad at all about everyone who died because of him?

I watched Dana turn a corner and then the elevator clunked to a stop.

"Well, are you coming?" she called out.

The elevator door creaked open. I poked my head in to peer up at the mirror that hung from the far corner of the ceiling. It was there so that before you stepped inside you could tell whether someone was hiding in the elevator—someone dangerous who might hurt you. There was no one. I stepped quietly in and pushed the button for my floor.

And that is how we stopped being friends.

GRE

When I was fourteen, my mother decided to apply to graduate school, and she asked me to help her study for the math portion of her GRE exams. At the time, I was studying geometry in school. Geometry was all about logic and proving things. It was fantastic.

My mother didn't need to know proofs, but I could see she was in trouble with what she did need to know. We sat in the kitchen, at our round white table, with my mother's scrap paper, pencils, and a thick book with problems and explanations and practice tests. She had a glass of Jack Daniels within reach.

My mother had worked for years as a case manager with Jewish Family Services, and now she wanted to become a psychologist. She didn't usually discuss her clients, because most of their stories were sad and complicated in ways she thought I wouldn't understand. "When you're older," she would say. Occasionally she shared something good that had happened to one or another of them. I especially liked to hear about the children. For example, a boy she liked had been caught shoplifting but now he was behaving himself, and my mother had helped him join a Boy Scout troop. He had recently earned a community service badge by helping an elderly neighbor with his grocery shopping.

My mother held onto the page as she read the explanation for how to do a certain type of word problem— a rate problem. Her hand was poised to turn the page as soon as she started to read. I thought that was her problem: she was in too much of a hurry. When I was younger, she would sometimes read the same book I was reading so we could talk about it together. At first, I was amazed by how fast she could read, but if I asked her about a particular character or part of the book, she never quite remembered. She read too fast—not actually reading but skimming. You can't skim math. You have to slow down and think about it, really take in all the information so that you're holding the whole thing altogether inside your head. At least that's how I did it.

As my mother read, I glanced around the kitchen and my eyes landed on the phone. She recently had a new phone line installed. The man from the phone company who did the installation—one in the kitchen, and one in my parents' bedroom—was cheerful and friendly. He wore blue pants and a matching blue shirt with his name, LOU, on a tag pinned to his chest. Lou seemed pretty relaxed. He didn't appear to worry about the little piles of plaster dust accumulating at the base of the walls where he drilled holes to insert the new phone wire, and he didn't mind us watching him work. From time to time he offered the scraps of phone wire he clipped off—pretty multi-colored bundles—to my younger sister Leah and me. After testing the lines out with an oversized handset that made sounds of differing frequencies, Lou had us listen to the two different rings—our old, familiar one, and a higher-pitched, louder, unpleasant ring that was the new line. Before he left he gave us a cursory lesson in how to access the two lines, without really waiting to see if any of us followed what he was doing.

"See," Lou said. "You punch here for your four-two-six-oh, here for your five-one-eight-three, here's your hold, you gotta punch the hold in between or you'll disconnect. These other buttons are blanks." He repeated the sequence a few times, and said, "Easy. You'll get the hang of it," but he didn't actually offer us a turn under his supervision. We couldn't wait to punch the buttons. Lou made it look fun.

"Okay, Naomi, I'm ready to get down to work," my mother said. I turned back to face her and watched her flip the page. "Let's find one of those rate problems." She slid the book over to me and while I looked through to find a problem, she took a sip of her bourbon. I have never liked the smell of it. I was looking for a simple problem without currents or tailwinds or two people leaving from two different points. It was best to start with a simple one.

"Okay," I said. "I've got one. 'Sally drives from New York to Boston, a distance of 220 miles. If it takes her 4 hours, and she does not stop along the way, what is her average speed?'"

My mother tapped her mauve-painted fingernails on the table. Lately she had stopped wearing her wedding ring. Sometimes a blood vessel would spontaneously burst in one of her fingers and then her finger would turn purple and swell up and I guess the ring would become too tight.

She had to stop wearing it until they figured out why this kept happening. They thought it might be a vitamin K or C deficiency, or something else entirely. I wasn't used to seeing her hand without the ring.

"I know there's a formula, let me look it up." She pulled the book close and thumbed through the pages she had just been reading, humming a little as she did so. "Okay, here it is, distance equals rate times time."

She took another sip of bourbon. "This is the last hurdle," she said. "Once I pass this math test, I'll be set." She looked up at the clock. "I have to get going on dinner in a few minutes. Maybe you could start cutting up the broccoli."

"Should I explain the formula to you?"

"Distance equals rate times time." She mumbled it a few times, trying to memorize it. "Why don't you explain it? Wait." She picked up a pencil and held it so the tip rested on a piece of blank paper.

"Well, the formula refers to a relationship between three things: how far you travel—that's the distance, how fast you move—that's the rate, or the speed, and how long you've been traveling—that's the time."

She wrote down, "1. How far. 2. How fast. 3. How long."

"So, for instance," I continued, "if you drove at sixty miles per hour and you went for an hour, what distance have you traveled?"

"Sixty miles per hour for an hour? That would just be an hour. I mean that would just be sixty miles. That's easy."

"And what if you traveled for two hours?"

"At sixty miles per hour?"

"Yes."

"A hundred and twenty miles."

"And how did you get that?"

"Is it right?"

"Yes. But how did you figure that out? Did you multiply?"

She thought for a minute. "I added."

"Well, multiplication is a shortcut for repeated addition. What if it had been five hours instead of two?"

"Five hours? Sixty for the first and sixty for the second, etcetera?"

"Yes."

My mother glanced at the clock again, then paused, pressing fingers and thumb together as though doing the eensie-weensie spider with one hand. "Three hundred miles?"

"Yes. Good."

"But I added it. I didn't multiply." She took another sip of bourbon. "I should start dinner in about five minutes."

"You added it, but you could have multiplied sixty times five."

"Oh, I see. I guess that works," she said with hesitation.

"So that's the formula. Rate times time equals distance. Should we look at the problem now?"

She wrote the formula on a piece of blank paper: rate times time equals distance. "Yes. Maybe two minutes."

"Sally drives a distance of 220 miles, and it takes her four hours. What is her average speed?"

My mother found the problem in the book and read it to herself over and over. She wrote down, "NY to Boston—220 miles."

"Boston," she said, formulating an idea. "You know, sometimes there are conferences up in Boston. Do you think you would manage okay if I went away for a weekend to a conference?"

I looked at her. It was not uncommon for my mother to take leaps of thought with no notice.

"I mean, Daddy would be here with you, of course. But I might have to go away to a conference sometime."

"Can we do the problem?" I said, pointing with a pencil to the book.

"Right." She stared at the paper.

I stared at the row of plastic buttons on the wall across from me, directly beneath the phone. Lou hadn't matched the color of the box right, the box that held the buttons. The phone itself was a cream color, and the button box was more of a beige. The buttons were fun to push, but we weren't allowed to answer the new line at all, even if my mother was not at home. *Especially* if my mother was not at home. She needed a phone line that was exclusively hers for her clients to use when she wasn't at the agency. I wasn't sure why my mother was so insistent about us not answering the new line. I would have thought it would be better just to take a message if somebody called. My mother said she needed to respect the privacy rights of her clients.

"This is different than the ones you asked me," she finally said.

"Well, there is a relationship between three things in this formula, and so every problem will always give you two of those things and ask you to find the third."

"Oh, I see. Oh, okay, I understand. So the distance is 220 miles and the time is 4 hours. Is average speed the rate?"

"Yes, good."

My mother looked at the clock again. "Maybe we should stop here so I can make dinner."

"Why don't you just finish this one problem? You're close."

My mother stared at the page again.

The day after we got the phone, I was in the kitchen getting a snack after school and the phone rang—our old, usual phone. I wasn't sure where Leah was—we were the only ones at home—but she didn't seem to be answering it, so I stared at the buttons, one of which was flashing, and then just picked up the phone.

"Hello?"

"Hi!" said the cheerful voice at the other end. It was Leah.

"Where are you?" I was quite puzzled.

"In Mommy and Daddy's bedroom. I'm calling you from the new line. Isn't this cool? Now we can talk on the phone to each other."

"That's ridiculous. Anyway, we're not supposed to use that phone."

"Hey, if we both walk out into the hall, we can see each other while we're talking. I'm walking now. I'm at their closets—I think it's going to reach—it is! Why aren't you in the hall?"

"I can't talk right now," I said. "I'm busy."

"I can't really concentrate right now," my mother said. "I have to make dinner." She put her pencil down, noticed a place where her nail polish was chipping and started to pick at it. "But I did well with the other ones, didn't I?"

I thought, wait till we get to headwinds and tailwinds,

or two people leaving from different places, meeting each other somewhere. Or one leaving before the other, and the second catching up and overtaking the first. There were a lot of problems my mother was going to have difficulty with. "Yes, you did those very well," I said.

She started to clear away the paper and pencils, and the book. "I'm really getting this, aren't I? I think I'm going to pass this test." She drained the last of her bourbon and considered her glass before putting it in the sink. "Why don't you go do your homework now, while I make dinner?"

I made my way down the black and white linoleum tiles in the hallway to the bedroom I shared with Leah. A couple of the tiles had started to curl up at the corner and I walked slowly so as not to stub a toe. I could hear the phone ringing. It was unmistakably the odd, high-pitched ring of the new line.

My mother picked up the phone and said hello, and then she said, "I just had such a fabulous idea. Hang on." She slid the pocket door shut, and I couldn't hear any more.

In our bedroom, Leah was trying to coax our cat Pinklepurr out from under her bed. I sat down on my own bed, with my math notebook. From where I sat, I could see Pinklepurr's black and white paw poking out from beneath the blue bedspread, reaching for the treat Leah was holding out. "Hey Pinkle puppy, here it is, good yummy treat." She had begun to call him 'puppy,' even though he was a cat. Leah really wanted a dog, but for many reasons having to do with who was going to walk it twice a day and who was going to pay for shots and heartworm pills, my parents would not let her have one. So lately she had started to train Pinklepurr to do the kinds of things a dog would do: sit, lie down, roll over, beg. She bought the cat treats with her own money. Actually, we weren't supposed to have food in our room.

"Training going well?" I asked.

"It was going great until the phone rang and he darted under the bed. He hates the sound of that ring."

"Fetch," I said.

"Fetch?"

"You should teach him to fetch, isn't that a dog thing? Then you could throw something across the room, and say, 'Fetch,' and he would come out from under the bed to get it. You should definitely work on the fetch command with him. It could prove very useful." Leah knew I didn't think much of her training Pinklepurr.

I thumbed through my math notebook. I was trying to write a direct proof that the angle bisectors of the base angles of an isosceles triangle would always bisect the perpendicular drawn from the third vertex. I had pages upon pages of drawings of triangles with many added lines and marks, everything all labeled, and strings of deductive steps written out with abbreviated justifications alongside each step. Once my geometry teacher had written on my homework, "You certainly know how to write a good proof. Also, a bad one that looks good." There was satisfaction in the writing of a proof, good or bad. I turned my notebook to a clean sheet, drew another triangle, and began to draw more lines inside it. Leah gave up on Pinklepurr.

"Why does Mommy have to take a math test?" she asked.

"She needs it to go back to school."

"What if she doesn't pass the test?" Leah picked up her *Handbook of Dog Breeds* and looked at the photographs inside.

"I don't know. I guess she couldn't go back to school, then."

"Then she'd have more time with us?"

"Well..." I drew a big X through the triangle I had been working on and turned to a clean page.

"I hope she doesn't pass the test."

"You better not say that to her."

Pinklepurr emerged from under Leah's bed. He was a big, fat, black and white cat. He always looked especially good when sitting on the tiles in the hallway. Leah stroked his head.

"She might have to go away sometime for a weekend," I said.

"She might? Who'll take care of us?"

"Daddy."

"Daddy? He doesn't know how to cook."

"Poor Daddy," I said.

"Why poor Daddy? Poor us."

"He would be lonely without Mommy here."

Leah turned back to her dog book, and I to my triangle. I was close to a proof, but I was missing one important step. After some time, the phone began to ring again. It was the sharp ring of the second line.

"Why isn't Mommy answering that phone?" asked Leah. She grabbed on to Pinklepurr, who looked ready to bolt again. "Should we get it?"

"I don't think so." I put my pencil down. "She said not to."

"Is Daddy allowed to answer the phone?" Leah asked.

I stood up. "That phone makes no sense. I'm gonna see why she's not answering it."

My mother was no longer in the kitchen. I looked at the phone. The ring was even louder from in there. I hated the sound. Could it hurt to pick it up? I put my hand on the receiver and stared at the flashing button, but I didn't lift it from the cradle. The ringing stopped. I looked around the kitchen. It didn't look like my mother had made much progress on dinner.

My parents' bedroom was empty. I walked over to the closed door of the bathroom and knocked on the door. "Mom?"

"What is it? I'm on the toilet."

"Mom, your phone has been ringing." She opened the door a crack. "Did you answer it?" she accused.

"No. I'm just telling you that it was ringing. We were wondering why *you* didn't answer it."

"I didn't hear it."

"I thought—"

"Wait." She closed the door, and I sat down on the bed to wait for her. I pulled her pillow out and propped it up against the wall. I was always a little wary of the black dye stains on her satin pillowcase. My mother hated it whenever I said she dyed her hair—she claimed that she didn't dye it—she rinsed it. I couldn't see the difference. Beside her bed was a night table with a phone on it, a new beige one with a row of buttons built right in. I started to push the buttons as though I were doing a finger exercise on the piano. Then I noticed there was a switch on the side that said: "On—off." It was switched to off.

The toilet flushed, and I heard the water running in the sink. When she came out of the bathroom, she looked like she might have been crying. She had freshened her lipstick. "Are you okay? Were you crying?"

"I'm just under a lot of stress right now. I'm juggling a lot of things."

"Well, I figured out about your phone."

My mother sat down slowly at the edge of the bed. "You figured something out about the phone? What did you figure out?"

"Why you didn't hear the phone ringing. I think the ringer was off on your phone."

"The ringer was off?" She seemed suddenly cheerful. "How do you know?"

"See." I showed her the switch. "Should I turn it on for you?"

"Thank you."

"What if the phone rings again? Can I pick it up?"

"No."

"I'm trying to help you—"

"You do help me. I'm telling you, we will get used to the phone... and everything else."

The phone rang again, the new line. My mother hurried over and picked it up. "Hello? One second." She held the phone against her chest. "Leave the room please, Naomi. And close the door behind you." She shooed me with her hand.

I stood just outside her door in the hallway, but I couldn't hear anything. Pinklepurr found me and sniffed at my ankles. I walked back to the kitchen, with Pinklepurr following. Leah joined us. "He's hungry," she said.

"After eating all those treats?"

"Well, I'm hungry," said Leah. "Did Mommy make dinner yet?" She looked around. The raw broccoli was on the cutting board only partially cut up. "Why didn't she make dinner? Where is she?"

"She's on the phone with a client," I answered. "I think it's a client." Then the phone started to ring again, but it was the old line, with the old usual ring.

"Now what do we do?"

"We answer it," I said.

"How?"

One button was lit, one was flashing.

"I guess you just pick it up," I said, reaching for the phone. I put the phone to my ear, but before I could say "hello," I heard my mother's voice say, "...didn't mean we should go to Boston, it just gave me the idea."

I quickly hung up. My heart was beating fast. The ringing continued.

"What happened?" asked Leah.

"I must have done it wrong. I don't know—those buttons..."

"Let me see." Leah pushed closer to the phone. "Oh, I get it," she said, and pushed the button that was flashing, then picked up the phone. "Hello?" she said. I stared at her, with a question on my face.

"It's okay," she said to me, triumphant. "It's for me."

Pinklepurr brushed against my legs. As I bent down to stroke his back, a piece of paper floated to the floor. I looked at my mother's sprawling loopy cursive. "1. How far. 2. How fast. 3. How long. Rate times time equals distance. New York to Boston—220 miles." She had underlined and circled the word "Boston." Something about her handwriting—so familiar to me—made me feel sad. I wasn't exactly sure why, but it was too big—too optimistic, maybe, and too incautious.

I sat down at the table and reached for the cutting board—somebody needed to finish cutting the broccoli—but then I noticed the GRE book that my mother had pushed aside, and I went for that instead.

In the back of the book there was an appendix of especially challenging word problems. I scanned a page, settled on a problem, and began to enter it with my mind.

L.A. SUMMER

The summer after high school I went to live in L.A. with my aunt Sharon and my cousin Beth. I was eighteen, set to go to college in the fall, had grown up in New York City and had never before been west of New Jersey. What I knew in advance about California came mostly from the Woody Allen movie *Play It Again, Sam*. Now I had been lifted out of my own life and into my aunt Sharon's world, in particular the world of Sharon's theater group, which they called "The Actors' Warehouse." The group had recently leased a warehouse off Cahuenga Boulevard to use as a theater (hence the name). The first night that I arrived in L.A. Sharon brought me over to the warehouse to meet everybody.

"This is my niece, Naomi," she announced. "She's staying with me for the summer and she wants to help out at the theater." Everyone welcomed me warmly, and Amy, the director of the group and of their first play, in which Sharon had a leading role, invited me to come to rehearsals and to participate in the yoga classes and other classes held at the theater. I felt shy but happy.

Afternoons, while Sharon worked as an occupational therapist and my cousin Beth was working as a CIT at a day camp, I spent time at the warehouse helping to build the interior of the theater. Johnny, the caretaker at my aunt's apartment complex, was in charge of the project, and his boyfriend Lenny helped out. They lived together in an apartment in the complex and I would drive over to the warehouse with them in their Wrangler Jeep with its top down. When they were stopped at red lights sometimes Johnny, the younger and more dramatic of the two, would reach over and grab Lenny's head in his two hands and plant a big kiss on his mouth. From the back seat, in the dungaree overalls I always wore, I liked imagining that anyone who saw them would also notice me and wonder who I was and how I had become friends with them.

I had always been shy altogether and even more so around adults, and I still felt shy, but these adults were different. Not just Johnny and Lenny, but all the members of the theater group. They were not like the parents of my friends. When Sharon introduced me, they all gave me big smiles, but they didn't grill me about my life and interests and they didn't need me to say anything. Lenny even once said to me that one of the things he liked about me was how quiet I was. They were actors, and I was an appreciative audience, a role I felt very comfortable in. Nobody there was my age and that was a relief. In high school I hadn't found a way to fit in, and now I didn't have to try. I didn't exactly fit in, but they made me feel I was a part of the group.

Johnny taught me how to do all kinds of things, like measure and cut the metal studs to size, use the electric screwdriver to fasten the pieces into a frame, and put together electrical plugs for the lighting booth. I also smoked pot for the first time in my life with him and Lenny. At one point Johnny pulled out a joint while they were taking a break and he held out his hand, offering it to me. I declined.

"You don't want a hit?"

"Well," I confessed. "I've never tried it. I don't know how."

He laughed. "I can teach you. It's really quite simple." I liked the feeling of sucking the air and the smoke together deep into my lungs, and how the marijuana made me feel relaxed and a little off-center. Johnny had pulled out a big wrench with red plastic handles to use as a roach clip and complimented me as I held it to my lips, "Very natural," he said. "You look very very cool. Doesn't Naomi look so cool, Lenny?"

In addition to helping Johnny and Lenny, I started going to yoga classes, and I also went to all the rehearsals of the play. At one rehearsal Amy, the director, lead Sharon and the other actors in an exercise to help them explore their characters. She asked them all kinds of questions about their likes and dislikes and fears and younger selves and work life and family life. I found it fascinating. I wished that I could be one of those actors. Not that I had any interest in performing on a stage—that was the last thing I could picture myself doing—but I imagined Amy scrutinizing me with those intense blue eyes, her head tipped to one side, asking me questions and listening and nodding as she took in the answers. I wanted to be under that microscope of Amy. I wished I could invent a character for myself and pretend to be that person and be interrogated by Amy.

Recently I had also taken on the responsibility of making curtains, not the stage ones, but those separating the audience section of the theater from the lighting booth and front office. At yoga class one day, Amy came in with some lush red velvet material that she had found in a dumpster somewhere. During the break Amy called out, "Does anyone know how to sew?" No one responded. "I found this great material we can use to make curtains for the lobby," she continued, "and I'll help, but I don't know enough to be in charge." Everyone remained silent. I didn't really like to sew, and didn't have much experience doing it, but I did know how. I had been forced to sew my sixth-grade graduation dress and also to sew a skirt in home-ec in eighth grade. I never imagined that I would, if given a choice, actually choose to take on a sewing project. However, there was something about Amy—I felt quite drawn to her. Making curtains together would be a way to get to spend some time alone with her. And how hard could it be to sew curtains? So I volunteered. "Thank you so much!" said Amy as she gave me a big smile.

We made a date to meet at the warehouse at ten o'clock the next Tuesday morning. It was fairly dark inside, the sunlight struggling to make its way through the few small, dirty windows. Metal studs formed the outline of walls yet to be built. Amy flipped on the light switch. The bank of dim fluorescent lights didn't help much.

Amy seemed quite relaxed, in a theatrical sort of way. That is, she sank into the cement floor, as much as that was possible, flopped her cloth bag down next to her and as her loose flowered cotton skirt parachuted to the floor, spread her hands behind her and leaned back a bit so that she had to tilt her head to look up at me. Amy was in her early forties, very tan with frosted hair that spun off in waves about her face. She had startlingly blue eyes—pained eyes—and very fine facial contours. Her smile revealed two rows of very white, perfectly even teeth. "Where do we start?"

"Well, we need to measure, the uh, material. I guess, uh, Johnny helped me figure out the dimensions we need for the curtains, so we just have to measure the, uh, material."

I changed positions on the cement floor, regretting that I hadn't thought to bring my yoga pad. "We need to calculate in for the hem and the, uh, part at the top that the rod goes through. So we start by measuring the material, I guess, measuring it off." I was aware that I was repeating myself. Also that I was close to inarticulate. But Amy didn't seem to care. She nodded intently at everything I said.

We spread the material out on the floor, and Amy found the yellow cloth tape measure in her bag. I had Amy set one end down at the edge of the red velvet, and then, on hands and knees, I laid the tape measure out across the length of the material as I crawled, flattening it with my hands. The velvet was smooth and soft to the touch. The straps of my dungaree overalls dug into my shoulders as I inched along.

Having marked off the lengths that we needed, I began to cut the material, while Amy set up the sewing machine. The last time I had sewn anything was in eighth grade when I had almost flunked home economics. All the girls in my class had to sew a skirt before we could work on any other projects, and, uninterested in the skirt—I always wore pants—I approached it with aggressive meticulousness. I was determined to do it all precisely right, which meant very slowly. It didn't matter to me if it took me all year to make one skirt, which is in fact what happened. Could I be faulted for being so attentive to detail? I would sit in class, placing each pin in the material just so, and if it went in at an angle instead of straight, I patiently removed it and set it in again. When I sewed a seam that wasn't absolutely straight I would rip it out and try again. It drove my teacher crazy.

Now Amy and I each finished our tasks, and I stood and stretched my back from side to side.

"Good idea," said Amy, imitating me.

"We're ready to pin them, I guess." I demonstrated how to pin the material.

Amy fumbled in her cloth bag for a pair of reading glasses. We sat in a rhythmic silence with a plastic box of straight pins between us, each with a heap of red velvet in her lap. Then Amy startled me with a question.

"Naomi, have you ever really loved? Do you think you know how to love?"

I blushed. This was a topic that embarrassed me. I had often wondered if something was wrong with me. While others in high school had started to date and become involved, and I knew some kids went so far as to sleep with each other, I had never even kissed a boy.

"I'm not sure what you mean. I mean, what kind of love? Have *you* ever loved anyone?"

Amy stopped pinning and looked straight at me. "I loved my father when I was a little girl, but then he died. I don't think I've allowed myself to love since then, since I was twelve years old. I don't think I know how to love."

I was surprised to find myself in the middle of a conversation that I had sometimes imagined I might have. Intense. Deep. Not even a preliminary, what college will you be going to, what are you going to major in? I had wanted to have a conversation like this but wasn't sure I was up to its demands. Should I be saying something about my own father? I didn't really want to talk about him. Of course I loved him, but recently everything had gotten more complicated with my parents. Would it be okay to ask how Amy's father had died? Amy continued to look expectantly at me, with those pained eyes, over the top rim of her glasses.

"I'm sorry about your father. That sounds hard, him dying when you were so young." That sounded stupid, but too late. I then remembered that Amy was married. I met Amy's husband once when he stopped by the theater to drop something off. He seemed nice. Did she mean she didn't love him? I thought that might be too forward to ask, but Amy had started this conversation. "Don't you, you didn't, I mean, didn't you ever love your husband?"

Amy shook her head. "I don't think I've ever really loved him. He's a very kind man, but I don't think I've allowed myself to love him."

I took this in. Did I think I didn't know how to love? If anything, what I doubted was not whether I could love but whether anyone would ever love me. Would it sound silly, young, to say that to Amy?

"I guess I think I would be able to love, but I've never been sure that anybody would love me. That's the thing I'm not sure about." I looked shyly down at the red velvet blanket covering my lap.

"Oh, I think you'll be loved. I'm certain you'll be loved."

Amy kept her eyes on me. I looked up at her but could only hold the gaze for a brief moment before attending to my curtain.

"The thing is," Amy resumed, "I feel that if only I could somehow talk to my father, it would free me to love someone else. In a crazy way I think I need his permission. The green light. I think I have this strange idea in my head that it would be a betrayal of him, to love someone else. So if he could tell me it wasn't, that he didn't mind, I could move forward."

I considered what Amy had just said. It was going to be hard for Amy to talk to a dead man. Well, easy to talk to, hard to get a response from.

"I mean I think originally I decided on some level never to love anyone else because it hurt so much when he died. But then it turned into a kind of loyalty thing. If I could hear him say, go ahead, love somebody, I think I could do it." She took her glasses off and dropped the pin she had been holding back in the box. "You know, there are people who say that if you want something you just have to ask for it over and over to yourself, keep asking, and it will happen. Like my friend Nora told me she was interested in meeting this guy she had seen at a movie—she didn't know him at all, she had just noticed him at the movie theater and felt interested—and so she started saying, 'Please let me meet the man from the movie,' over and over. You're supposed to say it in a request like that—please let something or other happen—and the next day she was trying to get a newspaper out of one of those metal stands, which she doesn't usually do—she usually buys her newspapers at the stationery store—only just that one day she didn't for some reason, and anyway it was stuck, the stand, and as she was pulling at it, the man from the movie happened to come by and offered to help her." Amy put her glasses back on, picked up another pin and started pinning the curtain again. "So I think about doing that. That is, just saying that over and over, 'Please let my father come talk to me,' but I don't know... I'm not sure it would work."

I had heard that people from California believed in these kinds of things. Even my cousin Beth, who was a pretty cynical fourteen-year-old, had a Ouija board she fooled around with occasionally. Lately she and a friend had been contacting President Kennedy, to ask him who was going to win the upcoming election.

"I have an idea," I said. "Would you be interested in trying to reach your father with a Ouija board?"

"Do you know how to use one? Do you have one?"

"Beth does. Maybe I could borrow it. Do you want to try?"

"I thought you might be able to help me with this. I don't know why. You know, I've never talked with anyone else about this, but I thought somehow, you would be the one who could... should we do it here? I think this place is the right place. Let's do it here, in the morning, like this. Nobody's here in the morning. Maybe on Thursday? Nine o'clock? Could you do it then?"

That Thursday morning was bright and sunny like every other summer morning in southern California. I caught a bus on Cahuenga Boulevard and met Amy outside the warehouse door, blinking my eyes as together we stepped into the cool, dimly lit cave. I had remembered to bring a towel so that we could sit more comfortably on the cement floor, and she laid it down in the middle of what was going to be the stage, once the theater was built, and placed the board in the middle of it. Some props were scattered about from the play that was in rehearsal: a few books, a couple of straight-backed chairs, a tea set. Amy had brought some candles and she placed them around the room, her hand shaking lightly as she lit each one. I was nervous, too, because although I was not a believer, I had participated the last time my cousin and her friend had played with the board, and I was surprised that the indicator really did seem to move around above the board as though being pulled by an unseen hand. I didn't know what was going to happen. I was also nervous about sitting so close to Amy in this hushed room. Our hands would probably touch.

"Why don't you sit down over there?" I pointed to one end of the towel. "Have you ever used one of these things before?" I sat down across the board from Amy. Her face was drained of color. She shook her head no, in a tight, constrained motion. "It's really pretty easy. We just place this indicator here in the middle of the board and put our hands lightly on top of it." I took a deep breath. We both reached out our hands and placed them gently atop the triangular wooden indicator with three small feet on the bottom, and a window of clear plastic.

"Now just think about your father. Just concentrate, and I'll ask if anyone is there." I paused, took another deep breath. The indicator remained still.

"Is anyone there?" We both stared down at the board. It was a rectangular board made of smooth blonde wood, about a foot and a half by two feet, with the word "yes" printed in black letters in the upper left-hand corner, "no" in the right, the alphabet spaced out in three slightly curving rows beneath, and the numbers zero through nine across the bottom. Very slowly the indicator seemed to come to life, to move hesitantly toward the "yes" corner. I had the same odd feeling that I had experienced with Beth. How did this work, anyway? Amy looked at me as I nodded gently in acknowledgment. When the indicator landed on the "yes" I said, "Is somebody there?" The indicator moved abruptly off and then back onto the "yes."

"Hello," I said. Amy whispered, "Hello." The indicator moved first to the "H," then to the "I," then a couple of times back and forth between the two.

"Hi, who are you? Can you tell us your name?" The indicator paused for a brief second, then spelled out "S-A-M."

"Sam? Your name is Sam?" The indicator careened toward "YES." Amy had trouble keeping her hands on top of it. "Well, hello, Sam. I'm Naomi." Once again Sam spelled out "H-I-H-I," then stopped. I looked at Amy, who swallowed.

"Is your father's name Sam?" I asked softly. Amy shook her head.

"Oh, so Sam isn't your father. Can I ask him about your father?"

Amy tried to speak but no words came out. She cleared her throat. "Yes. His name was Dan. Dan Steele. You can ask about him."

I was beginning to feel a little sorry for Amy, and more than a little sorry about having suggested doing this. I didn't believe in it myself, but still the feeling was rather remarkable. The indicator would move, and clearly nobody was moving it. At least not consciously. Amy looked solemnly down at the board. I had the impulse to reach over and push back the lock of hair that had fallen over her eye, but I refrained.

"Okay." Then louder: "Sam, this is Amy. Do you know Amy's father? Do you know Dan Steele?" The indicator moved up to the "yes."

"Is he there?" I felt Amy's hands tighten at the question. The indicator didn't move at first, but then slowly started making its way over to the "no." Halfway along the path it stopped, over blank territory, then started moving to the alphabet. "N." "O." "No?" I asked, but the indicator kept moving. "W." "Now?" The indicator repeated the three letters. "N-O-W." "Now? He's there now?" And the indicator lurched to the "yes."

"Does he have anything to say to Amy?" Amy was looking down, but her eyes were closed. I had a sudden urge to kiss her, gently, on the crown of her head. Meanwhile, the indicator had started to move. Slowly it spelled out, "LOVES AMY. DADDY LOVES AMY." Amy started to cry.

I felt she had gotten in a little over her head. "Should I stop now? Is this enough for now?" Amy nodded. Then as I was about to speak, Amy grabbed my hand.

"No, wait," she whispered. "I just want to say," she looked around her. "I love you, too, Daddy. I love you, too." The tears streamed down her cheeks.

"Okay, thanks Dan," I said. "And Sam. Thanks. We're going to say goodbye now. So long until next time." The indicator remained still. I waited a few minutes, then removed my hands. Amy followed suit. We sat very still, not looking at each other. I didn't know what to say, but I rummaged around in my overalls pocket for a clean tissue and offered it to Amy, who took it silently and wiped her cheek.

"Okay," she said. "Okay." And a few more times, "Okay." She paused, then after blowing her nose forcefully said, "Would you be willing to do this again?"

"Are you sure you want to do this again?"

"Well, I have to ask him. I didn't want to do it right then. It was too much, but now that I know I can talk to him, I have to ask him."

I didn't know what to believe, but I certainly didn't believe that Amy's father had really been there. "You know, I could borrow the board for you to use with someone else. Maybe you want to do this with your husband."

Amy stared at me, as I played with the loop on the right side of my overalls. "I think it has to be you."

I felt very nervous in my stomach. The fear was mixed with another feeling I couldn't identify. "Well, if you really think you want to. I guess I could do it again." I became aware that I had twisted the loop so tightly around my fingers they were turning white, and I wasn't sure how to extricate them.

"Next Thursday?" said Amy. "Nine o'clock again?"

"Okay," I said, still trying to disentangle my fingers from the loop on my overalls.

Yoga class met on Sunday mornings. This week it seemed the whole group was there. I felt a little awkward around Amy and tried to look at other people instead. I paid very close attention to Leila, the yoga teacher, who was a plump, gracious, courtly woman in her mid-fifties. I marveled that no matter what pose Leila assumed, she always looked as though she were sitting on a throne. Even, somehow, upside down on her head.

After class I went back home with Sharon, Johnny, and Lenny. We dropped Beth off at a friend's house and stopped to pick up some bagels on the way home. Back at the complex, Johnny placed some thick-cushioned chairs around a glass-topped table by the apartment pool, while Sharon went in to get some plates and knives and napkins. Lenny brought out a tray with glasses of juice and a vase of orange and yellow variegated tulips.

"Flowers! How beautiful! I would never have thought to do that," said Sharon.

Lenny shrugged shyly, and Johnny gave him a big kiss. We all sat down.

"What do you all think about Leila?" asked Sharon, as she played with a strand of her dark, thick, wavy hair. She wrapped it around and around her finger, let it go, repeated the motion. Sharon looked intently at the three of us.

"What do you mean, what do we think?" I asked. "She's great. Everyone thinks so."

Johnny nodded effusively. Johnny was a young twenty-five and had a mop of curly brown hair, which bounced now as he nodded. Lenny was thirty-two, balding and more sedate. "Yeah, Leila's cool," he said.

"I just think she's so wonderful," Sharon said, moonily.

"Well, what about it?" asked Johnny. Lenny laughed.

Sharon was puzzled. "What about it?" Then she gasped a little. "You mean you think I...?" I had noticed this about my aunt: Sharon loved a conversation in which it seemed another person knew something about her that she didn't. She was always excited to learn something about herself. "You think I, like, have a thing for Leila? You think I'm attracted to her?" Sharon giggled. Johnny and Lenny both nodded sagely. "You think so?" Sharon reached for her bagel. "Maybe I am. I never thought about it."

I was very interested in this conversation but I wished I could have been invisible. I looked down and began systematically to move my index finger about, intent on picking up every poppy seed that had fallen on my plate. My Aunt Sharon had had one husband already, Beth's father. They were divorced but she had dated other men over the years and recently had started dating someone new, Mickey. Could she be attracted to a woman and not have known it? The idea didn't seem to alarm her. She seemed to like it. But I doubted that she was going to stop dating Mickey. I really didn't understand how these things worked, how you knew what your feelings meant.

Johnny continued: "It seems as though you can't stop thinking about her. When we're in class you get this look on your face, looking at her, like she was a goddess."

"You're right! I do, because she moves so beautifully, and her voice is magic."

"See. Listen to how you talk about her. I mean, we all think Leila's great, but you have a certain tone when you talk about her." He continued in a falsetto: "Leila moves so beautifully." I glanced up at Johnny and saw that he had clasped both hands to his chest. Sharon burst out laughing. She was clearly enjoying the attention. I looked down again. I was thinking about Amy, wondering what kind of expression I had on my face when I looked at her.

That Thursday morning, I awoke early, feeling anxious. I was disturbed by the whole Ouija board thing. I didn't believe in it, but I didn't know how to explain it, either. I wondered if it had been me causing the indicator to move. Maybe my thoughts could somehow make it move, without my hand actually pushing it, and that thought scared me. My unconscious thoughts. I was afraid of what the indicator might reveal about what I was thinking. Like what if I had feelings about Amy? Well, it could just as likely be Amy's thoughts ruling it. More likely, in fact. I wished I understood how it worked.

At the theater, I lay down the towel and set out the Ouija board while Amy lit some candles. Amy cleared her throat a few times. "You know, I thought maybe you could speak first, you could contact that Sam person like last time, and see if my father is there, but then once we know my father is there, too, maybe I could just do the talking then."

"That's fine with me. I mean, you could do the whole thing if you wanted to, also."

"No, I think it would be good to begin it the same way as last time. It would be, like, somehow, ritualizing it." I wasn't sure what Amy meant, but I agreed.

We sat with our hands on the indicator. "Uh, Sam, uh, hello, Sam, are you there?" After a small pause, the indicator moved decisively over to the "yes." "Uh, hello." Amy echoed, "Hello." The indicator lurched to the "H," then back and forth several times between "H" and "I."

"Um, Sam, Amy wanted to talk to her father, Dan Steele. Is he there?" For a long minute nothing happened. I watched Amy concentrate on the indicator. Finally it seemed to begin to move, creeping its way slowly over to the "yes."

"Is that you, Daddy?"

The indicator moved away from, then sharply back to the "yes."

"Hello, Daddy." There was no response. A taciturn guy, this Dan Steele, I thought. Not that I actually believed this was Amy's father. I was concentrating on keeping my mind blank, trying not to think about anything at all, but that was hard to do. I had once read something about how some people who were being tortured repeated nursery rhymes to themselves. Or counted backwards. Anything to prevent entry into their minds. So in my head, I began to recite the thing that came to mind: "James James Morrison Morrison Weatherby George Dupree—"

"Daddy, I've been troubled all these years," Amy began. "I wasn't sure it would be okay to love anyone but you. So I wanted to ask you about it. I wanted you to tell me that you would be okay if I loved somebody else."

I looked at Amy, who was staring intently down at the indicator, talking right to it, as though the indicator were her father. A small, polished amethyst that hung from a silver chain around her neck bobbed gently back and forth as she leaned forward. I forced myself to look away from the hint of cleavage exposed by the tank top she was wearing. "Took great care of his mother, though he was only three..." The indicator slowly started to move toward the alphabet, landing on the "N."

"N?" Amy asked. The indicator paused on the "N" and then moved slowly to the next letter, "O."

"'O?'" Amy's voice rose in distress. "'N-O?' NO? You mean it's not ok? You don't want me to love someone else?" But then the indicator moved two letters down to the "M." And from there to the "I."

"Nomi? What does that mean?"

I blushed. "Actually, Nomi is my nickname. Not many people use it anymore."

"Do you mean Naomi? What about her?"

The indicator lurched under our hands and then moved steadily to spell out "LOVE."

"Love? Are you telling me it's okay to love somebody else?" Amy said.

As loudly as possible inside my own head, I continued, "James James said to his mother."

The indicator again spelled out "LOVE." And a third time: "LOVE."

"Mother he said, said he."

"Daddy, I think that's what you're telling me. That I should go ahead and love. Is there anything more you want to say?"

The indicator was still.

"Daddy?" Amy stared at the board. "I guess he's gone."

Amy left her hands on the indicator for some time after I took mine off. I watched a few slow tears slide down her cheek. "It's just that he didn't say goodbye. And it felt, I don't know, somehow cryptic. Incomplete. Although I guess I got an answer to my question."

"I think you did."

"But why did he begin with your name? What did that mean?"

I shrugged my shoulders. I was ready to leave the warehouse and get back to my aunt's apartment. The whole experience made me uncomfortable. I thought I knew why he had spelled out my name. I wanted to hide.

That night, at the play rehearsal, I kept my eyes on Amy as she sat watching the actors with an intent look on her face. Beautiful Amy. I thought about her friend Nora, who wanted to meet the man from the movie. Could it hurt to try? Slowly I began to repeat to myself, over and over, a single simple sentence: "Please let Amy love me. Please let Amy love me. Please let Amy love me."

ZEITGEIST

1. Actuarial Trainee

I would never have imagined myself as an actuarial trainee—in fact, I had never before even heard of an actuarial trainee—but in combing through the Sunday Times classified ads, "actuarial trainee" was the only entry-level job for math majors I could find that required no other practical skills or experience. I had graduated from college in January of 1979 knowing only that I wanted to live in Manhattan. I had no idea where I was headed in my life. I needed a job and an apartment. I figured that once I had those, I would see where life led me.

"You'll like it at IRI," said Mr. Harris, the employment agent who referred me to the Insurance Ratemaking Institute. He pronounced it, "eerie." "Lots of young people, right out of college. I just placed someone in September. You would like him. Long hair, beard. Very smart guy, that one. Went to Yale. Your type of guy." Then he made me promise him that when I went for my interview, I would wear a skirt. I didn't own a skirt.

The tall modern building with glistening glass windows was all the way down on Water St. in lower Manhattan, near the South St. Seaport Museum. It required a bus ride and three different subway lines to get there from my mother's apartment in the Bronx, where I was staying until I earned enough money to start looking for a place in Manhattan. I gave myself two hours to get there and it felt like an accomplishment just to find the place. Especially while wearing a borrowed skirt.

I was under the impression that I would first meet with someone in Human Resources and then with one of the department managers. The HR man described the company as though he were reciting the kind of rapidly spoken cautionary warning that comes at the end of a commercial for a pharmaceutical product: "The Insurance Ratemaking Institute is a provider of statistical, actuarial, underwriting, and claims information and analytics; compliance and fraud identification tools; policy language; information about specific locations; and technical services. We serve insurers, reinsurers, agents and brokers, insurance regulators, risk managers, and other participants in the property/casualty insurance marketplace." I expected him to close with, "not to be used by children or pregnant women without a doctor's advice."

"Questions?"

I had no idea what anything he said meant, and it all went by so quickly that I didn't even know how to begin to formulate a question. "Nope, no questions," I replied.

"So, we'd like to set up an interview for you with the manager of the actuarial department, Sheldon Rosenberg. Does this time next week work for you?"

"Uh, yes, that would be fine. Thank you."

Next week?

He handed me a little card with the name, date, and time written on it. "See you next week then."

"Yes, good, see you next week. Nice to meet you. Thank you."

I was polite but fuming inside. I couldn't believe I had traveled all this way in a skirt for a five-minute conversation only to have to come back again on another day for the interview. "Forget it," I thought to myself. "I'm never coming back here."

Later that afternoon Mr. Harris, the employment agent, called me at my mother's apartment. "Human Resources said he wasn't going to bring you upstairs the way you were dressed."

"But I was wearing a skirt like you told me to."

"Listen, he's on your side. When you go back you have to wear a business suit with a skirt and jacket and do something with your hair." My hair was long and frizzy. "Maybe put it up in a bun, off your face. Also no dangly earrings. He's doing you a favor. He thinks they would hire you if you looked right. So do what he says."

I thought it was ridiculous. Did they actually think that what you wore determined what you were capable of doing? That women would somehow lose their mental capabilities if they wore pants? Or the wrong skirt? I almost didn't go back, because it was clear I would never feel like I belonged in this place. I would never be entirely comfortable; I would always be forced to wear clothes that were alien to me. But I did want to live in Manhattan. And for that I needed a job.

2. Benjamin

The actuarial department of the Insurance Ratemaking Institute took up an entire floor of the building. The interior of the floor was laid out in a grid, with rectangular areas each containing six desks partitioned off by shoulder-height bookcases, three desks each on opposite sides with hallways running through the middle.

Benjamin and I were in different divisions and would never have met except that one day at lunchtime, after I'd been working there for a couple weeks, we happened to be waiting for the elevator at the same time. I knew this was the man Mr. Harris had mentioned. Someone else who didn't fit in at IRI. My type. Short with glasses and already balding, what hair he did have was indeed long, but straggly. The compensating beard was thick and dark. He was wearing ugly brown polyester pants that barely reached his ankles and a green, black, blue and white plaid jacket, too small for him, which he later explained had been his bar mitzvah jacket, the only one he owned. I myself was wearing a navy-blue suit and cream-colored blouse, with my hair pulled back in a bun. When I was hired, my mother cheerfully bought me two staid suits. Without her stating it explicitly, I could tell she was hopeful that I had turned some kind of corner, that somehow this job would transform me into someone other than the Naomi who never shaved her legs or armpits, never wore make-up, never straightened her hair, and never wore a dress.

The office building was sixteen stories high and the complicated queuing formula that determined the route for each of the three elevators often resulted in long waits.

Particularly at lunchtime. So Benjamin and I stood for several minutes while waiting for the "down" elevator. We said hi and I happened to mention I was a vegetarian. Benjamin nodded knowingly and said, "Me too," followed by something else I didn't entirely understand the meaning of, involving the word "zeitgeist." He wondered whether I knew of a particular falafel stand at the nearby South Street Seaport. It had already become my favorite lunch spot. We went there together that day, and on the walk over he amused me by attempting to hum a John Cage piece for prepared piano. I didn't know who John Cage was, and I had no idea what was meant by a prepared piano. Over lunch he told me all about the music he himself composed, mentioning in an off-hand way that he had already composed over a hundred pieces, excluding juvenilia. He really used that word, as though at twenty-one he was already mature. Nobody I knew would be able to stand this guy, I thought. Nevertheless, I liked him. There was something sweet about his eagerness to impress me.

A few weeks later we went to a concert at the performance space called The Kitchen. He had a membership that entitled him to two free passes for every event. We left the office together and first went to his apartment, a studio off Bleecker St. in the West Village. He lived in the rear of a double building that had a small courtyard in between. In order to get to his apartment, we entered the building closest to the street and then walked through the courtyard, where a small tree was growing, to the back building. His place was small, the sparsely furnished interior gloomy with walls painted a dingy grey-brown, but because the apartment was tucked back behind the street and because the single window looked out on the courtyard, I thought it was magical.

I went through the tiny galley kitchen into his bathroom to change out of my work clothes and release my hair from its bun. I emerged wearing sneakers, jeans, and an unbuttoned flannel shirt over my t-shirt. Benjamin was wearing almost the same outfit as mine

"Ahh, it's the true Naomi!" With a big smile he lifted and let drop a few strands of my long frizzy hair, as though draping tinsel on a Christmas tree, then spread his arms wide. We embraced. We had already been joking about how Mr. Harris—the employment agent—was our *shatkhn*, our matchmaker. At this moment it felt like we were meeting each other for the first time.

We ate lunch together every day, either at the falafel stand or walking the few blocks up to Chinatown, but I was still living in the Bronx with my mother so it wasn't easy to get together outside of work. About a month later, Benjamin clipped a Village Voice classified ad for an apartment at an affordable rent just a few blocks from his. It was a tiny place on the third floor of a five-story walk-up, with a view of the next building over, about three feet away. The kitchen had just room enough for a small table and a couple of chairs. There was no bathroom as such: instead, on one side of the kitchen sink was a curtained-off cubicle containing the toilet, and on the other side the shower. A platform bed had been built into the small brick-walled bedroom. It felt like a cocoon. I loved it.

We began to spend almost every evening together, going out for dinner and to performances, mostly at The Kitchen. We occasionally spent the night at his apartment or mine, but this was my first relationship and I wanted to go slowly. Benjamin was fine with that and told me I should set the pace.

The thing about being actuarial trainees was that we needed to take actuarial exams. In order to become an actual actuary you had to pass ten exams over the course of several years. They were offered twice a year. It was a big topic of conversation at IRI. Benjamin suggested that we get a motel room in Montauk for an intensive studying weekend right before the exams. It was early May. "Beaches," I thought. "Ocean."

Going to Montauk to study for the actuarial exams—it was not what you would call a romantic getaway. We left on a Friday after changing out of our work clothes and grabbing a couple of slices of pizza on the way to Penn Station. We took the Long Island Railroad, Benjamin carrying a backpack full of textbooks and no apparent change of clothes. He wanted to start right in on Bayes' theorem as soon as the train pulled out of the station, but I wanted only to sit and stare out the window. So instead he quietly reviewed the Theory of Interest by himself.

The motel was right near the ocean and there was indeed a beach. However, it poured the whole weekend. And Benjamin really had in mind a marathon of studying. I couldn't wait to get back home. I had loved math all my life, but my experience in college as one of the few female math majors in classrooms dominated by confident men had made me somewhat insecure when confronted with complex concepts that required some time to synthesize. I understood the cultural determinants of how I felt but my feminist analysis didn't really help—in fact, it made me feel doubly terrible whenever I experienced self-doubt because I knew I was succumbing to our sexist culture's gender expectations. Benjamin, although well-intentioned—also a feminist, wanting only to help me feel confident—made it all the worse through his unwavering belief in his own abilities and his relentless desire to teach me what he knew and I didn't. By midnight on Saturday, after his third gleeful try at explaining the Neyman/Pearson lemma, I began to cry.

"What's the matter? Is something wrong?" The motel room was dark and musty, with occasional lightning flashes casting shadows on the wall through the slats of the blinds, and the anticipation of the thunder to follow doing nothing to prevent the shock to my system when the loud crack would finally arrive. His books were sprawled out over the one double bed, which made it difficult to find a comfortable way to stretch out my legs.

"Is something wrong? I feel like shit. Like I'm in some kind of nightmare I can't wake up from. I don't even care about the stupid exams. I'm tired. I'm hungry. I don't want to be an actuary. I have no idea what I'm doing with my life."

Benjamin looked crestfallen. "I thought it would be fun to do this together."

"This is not my idea of fun," I sobbed. "I need to go to sleep."

"OK, you sleep."

"I can't sleep with your damn books all over the bed."

"OK, OK." He collected his books and made a stack on the floor over by his side of the bed. "You go to sleep now."

It seemed to me he spent the whole night studying because the next morning when I woke he was sitting up, a pillow behind him propped up against the headboard, his legs stretched out, and a math book on his thighs.

"Good morning," he said, ever cheerful, when I sat up. "I have a great idea."

I was wary of his great ideas.

"You do? Do you think I will think it's a great idea?"

"I'm sure you will."

That was not a surprise to me. "Does it have to do with studying for the exams?"

"It has nothing to do with the exams."

I felt better already. "OK, what is it?"

"I had this idea a little while ago, but I was waiting until after the exams to talk about it."

"Okay, so what is it?"

"I thought we could write an opera together."

I hadn't known what I expected him to say, but this was not it.

"Benjamin. You're a composer. I'm not a composer. Do you think you're going to teach me how to write music now? That's your idea? Do you really think that would be good for my self-esteem or for our friendship?"

"No, no, not at all. My idea is not to teach you composition. My idea is: I'm the composer, but you're the writer. I'll write the score, and you write the libretto."

I liked that idea better. I didn't exactly think of myself as a writer, but I had mentioned to Benjamin that I'd written some stories and was thinking about doing more of that.

"I've already figured out what the opera's about," he continued. Of course he had. "Galois. Evariste Galois, the French mathematician. About him and his mathematics."

I knew about Galois from ninth-grade geometry, because he had proved you can't trisect an angle with a ruler and compass. "Didn't he die at a young age fighting a duel or something?"

"Yes. I don't really know much about him, but I've been teaching myself Galois Theory. I already have some ideas about how to translate Galois' mathematical ideas into music."

"The duel thing does seem very operatic."

"Precisely. What do you think?"

I was a little bit intrigued. This could actually be a good idea. "I guess it might be fun. I should read something about him—about his life."

"Great. I thought we'd get started after the exams."

I paused. "Okay, sure, why not? These exams will soon be over. Sure, let's try it."

"And actually, I was thinking we would do a trilogy of operas about famous mathematicians. We could start with Galois, and then move on to Hypatia and Ramanujan."

That was so Benjamin.

We took the exams that week. It would take about six weeks for us to get the results.

So we turned to Galois.

3. Evariste Galois

Evariste Galois died in 1814 at the age of twenty in a duel of honor, fighting over a woman whom he didn't know well. He had stayed up the whole night before the morning of the duel, trying desperately to write all his mathematical ideas down on paper. He knew he was going to die. His mathematical ideas laid the foundation for a branch of abstract algebra called Galois Theory. In his short life Galois had a lot of bad luck. His father committed suicide. He himself was arrested in a barroom brawl for shouting out pro-Republic sentiments. He wasn't admitted to the *École Normale Supérieur*, because his examiners didn't recognize the talent in his cryptic answers so he failed the entrance exam. Starting at age fifteen he would send mathematical treatises to famous mathematicians like Gauss, but somehow they always got lost. He never once received a reply. He was in fact never recognized while alive. His was an operatic life.

Although interested in the events of Galois' life, Benjamin was mainly focused on Galois' mathematical ideas. He knew exactly how he would translate those ideas into music. In addition, he knew precisely how he wanted to stage the musicians so that the physical configurations would illustrate some of the algebraic structures that Galois had discovered. Benjamin and I soon ran into trouble trying to work on the opera together. In theory we were working together on the opera, but it turned out that really we were working quite separately. He was going along full steam with his music and I had not really found my bearings.

It was time for the exam results to be posted—a nervous time for some people because the scores could determine whether or not they would continue working there. The company didn't have an explicit three strikes and you're out policy, but it had ways to discourage people who repeatedly failed from pursuing the actuarial path. The employment cycle was therefore tied to the exam cycle. When the results came in, inevitably some people resigned. Job postings went out to the agencies, which then listed their advertisements in the classifieds.

Benjamin and I both succeeded in passing our exams. Those of us who were staying on were eager to see the new crop of actuarial trainees.

4. Sarah

We both noticed her. I spotted her even before she was hired, when she was leaving my manager's office after her interview. Something about her intrigued me, although I only saw her from behind. She was tall and slender and moved gracefully. Maybe it was her extremely short-cropped brown hair. Perhaps another misfit? A potential new friend?

A week later when I made my way over to Benjamin's cubicle during a morning break, there she was. I could hear Benjamin's voice as I approached. He had a tendency to speak loudly when explaining something, as though he were a professor standing at a podium giving a lecture. They were looking together at a rate report on his desk. She heard me coming and turned her head toward me as he kept speaking, oblivious that he had lost his audience. When I got close, he too looked up.

"Hi," he said to me. "Have you met Sarah? She's just started working in my division."

"No, I haven't." I nodded to her and held out my hand. "Hi, I'm Naomi. Welcome to IRI."

"Naomi works over in the research division," Benjamin explained to Sarah, "where I was hoping to be placed when I was hired. She gets to fool around with new methods of rate-making using econometrics, least-square regressions, that kind of thing, rather than having to churn out these cookie-cutter rate reports where we just plug numbers into the tired old formulae." He pointed to the report on his desk. I recognized his eagerness to impress her with his use of technical vocabulary. Somewhat like a peacock spreading its feathers.

"Benjamin makes my work sound more interesting

than it is," I said. "Unless you're one of the people for whom actuarial science is more than just a way to make a living." I smiled. I guess I was doing my own kind of signaling. Sarah smiled back.

We arranged to meet later for lunch. And from that day on, the three of us ate lunch together every day. Sarah was a modern—or a postmodern—dancer, who had also majored in math and had moved to the city to try to break into the dance world. It turned out that she had gone through the same employment agency that we had, and that Mr. Harris had described both Benjamin and me to her as "her type."

"At least I think it was you two he was describing," she said. "He told me the story about how they wouldn't let you go upstairs for your interview until you wore different clothes. And also about your hair."

"Show her your hair," Benjamin said, reaching for the bobby pins in my bun. I slapped his hand away and undid the bun myself. The cascades of my curly frizz fell over my shoulders and down my back.

"Such beautiful hair," Sarah said, reaching over to rake her fingers through it. "And so soft."

Little shivers spread from my head down to my toes. I didn't want her to stop touching my hair.

Benjamin had the idea to enlist Sarah to do the choreography for our Galois opera. At our next lunch, which was on a Friday, he brought it up. I told her what I knew about Galois's short life. She asked a few questions and seemed interested but needed some time to think about it. She had been very busy preparing for a dance performance that was happening that weekend at the Judson Memorial Church. A group of dancers was gathering for a performance of something called Contact Improvisation—including Steve Paxton, whose name she seemed to expect us to have heard of, but I hadn't. A year ago she had taken a workshop with him at her college, and she was excited that he invited her to be a part of this performance. Benjamin and I planned to go.

It was a big room with a wooden floor. The audience sat around the perimeter in a big oval while the dancers, about ten of them, huddled in the center as though forming a scrum. They began to move. The dance was without music. The only sounds were of bodies against bodies, or bodies against floor. A circle of bodies. Breaking into smaller groups of two or three, forming and reforming. Bodies falling upon bodies. Keeping contact. Flowing like a river. Or a glacier. Or in pulsing waves, like the ocean. Leaning. Giving weight. Taking weight. Slow. Languorous. Linking eyes with intense concentration. Smiles. Tears. And somehow the audience also a part of the dance. I felt like a newborn emerged into a world I knew nothing about. And I could not stop looking at Sarah, mesmerized by the way her body moved.

Afterwards Benjamin went over to say hi to a composer friend he had spotted across the room, and I found Sarah. We hugged.

"That was amazing," I said. "Beautiful."

"You liked it?" she asked shyly.

"I loved it. I had no idea..." A thought occurred to me. "Would you want to go out for dinner sometime after work? I would really like to hear all about your dancing life."

"Sure, I'd love that."

We smiled at each other.

"Thanks for coming to this," she said.

"I'm so glad I did. Really, really glad." I squeezed her hand goodbye.

At lunch on Monday Sarah told us she would like to do the choreography for the opera. She was thinking about basing the choreography on French dances of that time. Benjamin tried to explain how his music would be based not on the time period Galois lived in but on his mathematics. "That's fine," she said, "but if we're talking about Republican uprisings and duels, then wouldn't it make sense to reference the music and dance of that era?"

I enjoyed watching her challenge Benjamin's authority.

The next day she handed a long list to Benjamin of French dances that she was considering drawing on— *Bourrée, Canary, Chaconne, Courante, Entrée grave, Forlana, Gavotte, Gigue, Loure, Menuet, Musette,* and *Passacaille*—and told him she needed to know which of those dances he felt would best correspond to his compositions for each of the different parts of the opera.

Benjamin took the list but looked doubtful.

That night Benjamin said to me that he wasn't sure about Sarah doing the choreography for Galois.

The following week at lunch Sarah asked him if he had made any progress on her list of French dances.

"It's an interesting idea but I'm not sure it will integrate with my composition," said Benjamin.

"What does that mean?" asked Sarah.

"Well..." Then his face lit up. "Here's an idea. Maybe you could get started on one of the other operas."

"There are other operas?"

"We're actually planning to do a trilogy of operas

based on three different mathematicians," I offered.

"You're kidding me."

"No, it's for real," said Benjamin. "Hypatia and Ramanujan. Actually, you'd probably love thinking about those two. She was Greek. He was Indian. What do you think? Maybe Hypatia. I've got some notes I jotted down about some of her work on diophantine equations—some musical ideas I had. I can look them over and let you know where I think I'll be going with that."

5. Hypatia

Benjamin had a rare work deadline that meant he couldn't join us for lunch the next day. I had read about Hypatia the night before and while eating our falafel pockets, I filled Sarah in on what I learned.

"Hypatia was a Greek mathematician, philosopher and astronomer who lived in Alexandria from 370 to 415 A.D."

"Really? A woman could be a mathematician and a philosopher and an astronomer back then?"

"Yeah. She actually taught at the University of Alexandria and she not only wrote several mathematical treatises, but she also invented some scientific instruments."

"Anything I would have heard of?" asked Sarah.

"The astrolabe? Have you heard of that?"

"Wow, a woman invented the astrolabe? I had no idea."

"Yeah, and then she was killed."

"Killed by whom? Why?"

"By a mob of Christian religious fanatics, who were angry about her heretical neo-Platonic beliefs. They dragged her from her chariot while she was on her way to teach at the university."

"Wow," said Sarah. "A great subject for an opera. A feminist opera."

"Well, I guess."

"You don't think so?"

"I'm not sure how to say this, but there's something about Benjamin and these operas, well actually, something I'm trying to figure out about—oops..." I had jerked my arm away from my body to prevent the tahini sauce that was dripping out the bottom of my pita bread from landing on my skirt, but accidentally managed to fling some of it onto the sleeve of Sarah's dress instead. "Jesus I'm so sorry. That was stupid of me." I quickly ate the last few bites of my falafel pocket and then grabbed some napkins and tried to wipe her dress.

"Don't worry, I'm sure it'll wash out," Sarah said. "Look, for now I'll just roll up my sleeves. No one will notice." I watched as she rolled up her sleeves to reveal the shapely muscles of her forearms.

"What are you looking at?" asked Sarah.

"Nothing. I mean, I'm just admiring your arms. Strong arms. A dancer's arms." What I didn't say was the thought that had flashed through my mind—what would it feel like to be held in those arms?

Sarah looked at her watch. "I guess it's time to go back." We began to walk toward IRI.

"What were you starting to say before?" Sarah asked.

I was silent for a bit. "I don't remember."

"It was something about Benjamin and the operas? Or something you were trying to figure out?"

But by then we were at the entrance to our building, and in the crowds of people waiting for the elevators, it wasn't possible to continue the conversation.

That evening Benjamin was unusually quiet as we left work and set out to walk home. When we approached a traffic light, he turned to me.

"Naomi, this just isn't working," he said.

I was startled. Was Benjamin also having some doubts about our relationship? Was it really just going to end then, just like that?

"It's not working?" I asked, stalling to figure out what it was I wanted to say to him.

"It's not working. Hypatia's math just doesn't lend itself to any musical ideas. I thought I had written down some ideas for the Hypatia opera, but last night I looked at them and I'm afraid they're just not going to go anywhere."

Oh. I had almost just blurted out something about how I too felt it wasn't working—that my feelings for him had also been changing. I realized that Benjamin had no idea how I was feeling.

"I'm sorry," Benjamin tugged at his beard, a sure sign that he was nervous, "but I think that we should just focus on Galois. And I don't know what to do about Sarah."

"About Sarah?"

"I know that I was kind of negative about her ideas for the choreography and it might have seemed like I was ramming through my mathematical ideas about the music and the staging, but I think you'll really like what I've done. I'll soon be ready to play you some of it. It just doesn't work with any of her French dances." Benjamin kept tugging at his beard.

6. Ramanujan

Unsure of what I was feeling about Benjamin or Sarah or Galois or Hypatia, when I got home that evening I picked up the Ramanujan biographies I had checked out of the library and thumbed through them. Ramanujan was born in India in 1887 and became excited about mathematics at a very young age. Although admitted to the university he soon flunked out because he refused to study anything other than mathematics. Poor and desolate, he did manage to meet up with some Indian mathematicians who encouraged him to write to some British mathematicians, and at the age of twenty-six he wrote a letter to the British mathematician G.H. Hardy, at Cambridge University. He sent Hardy over one hundred original theorems. It took Hardy no time at all to determine that Ramanujan was a genius, and he encouraged Ramanujan to come to Cambridge to study. After some resistance, Ramanujan did so. He spent three years working with Hardy. During that time he suffered from the cold winters, had difficulty finding vegetarian food, and contracted an undiagnosed illness from which, at age thirty-two, he died.

Of all that I read about Ramanujan, the thing that struck me the most was that every single biographer mentioned his difficulty finding vegetarian food in England. Clearly they all believed this was of some importance. I was a vegetarian and sympathetic. I also had been eating Indian food frequently since Benjamin had introduced me to it the first night we had dinner together. I understood the unique craving one could have for that cuisine. I thought about making a kind of Sensurround opera, where the opera hall would be filled with the smells of Indian cooking, and Ramanujan would spend the entire opera sniffing and longing, but never finding a good meal.

The next day at work it was hard to focus. I could think only about food: Indian food, French food, Greek food. Maybe instead of operas we could do a trilogy of restaurants. In fact, why stop at three? We could open up a chain of vegetarian restaurants, each named for a different mathematician, each specializing in a different cuisine. Finally, it was time to break for lunch.

I told Sarah and Benjamin what I had learned about Ramanujan.

"Hmm..." said Sarah. "Indian dance. That could be fun."

"Do you want to start thinking about it?" suggested Benjamin.

"I thought you said that you had some notes about the music for the Hypatia opera and I could start working on that one."

"Yeah, but if you're drawn to Indian dance—you could just go ahead and begin thinking about Ramanujan."

"Isn't that kind of like putting the cart before the horse?" said Sarah. "To start with the choreography before the music is written? And anyway I'm still waiting to hear your ideas about where I should go with the Galois. Whether there's some kind of choreography you think would quote 'integrate with your composition.'" She signaled quote marks with her fingers as she spoke the last phrase. Benjamin looked down at his sandwich and took a bite.

The conversation was making me uncomfortable.

"Did either of you ever think about which one of these mathematicians you identify with?" I said.

Sarah laughed. She counted off with her fingers. "Killed in a duel, attacked by a mob, starved to death. Take your pick."

"No, I'm serious," I said.

Benjamin stared at me. "What do you mean? I have no idea how to even begin to answer that question. Wouldn't it be kind of hubris?"

"I don't mean their mathematical genius. It's just that for some reason I found myself identifying with Galois."

"With Galois?" Benjamin said. "That I really don't understand. I might have thought you would say Hypatia— I mean she was a woman."

"No, I don't mean that. It's just something about how nothing ever turned out well for him. His father's suicide, and failing that entrance exam, and getting arrested standing up for the Republic, and all those letters he sent that never reached their destination, and then getting killed for a woman he doesn't even love. He was kind of a lost soul."

"And you feel like you're a lost soul?" asked Benjamin.

"Not really." I shrugged. "I can't explain it. There's just something that resonates for me."

Sarah stood up. "I hate to end this fascinating conversation but it's time to get back to work."

When we got off the elevator Sarah and I dipped into the restroom before heading to our desks. As we stood at the sinks washing our hands, Sarah said, "Can I ask you a question?"

"Sure."

"What is going on with these operas? Are they really going to happen? All three of them?"

"Oh God," I said. "I don't know. I think you should ask

Benjamin that question."

"Are you enjoying working on them?"

"I'm not really doing much—it's Benjamin who's been spending a lot of time studying Galois Theory and working on the music. He's really excited about what he's been doing, but I haven't heard any of it yet." I shook my wet hands over the sink and went over to the paper towel dispenser. "It was his idea. The operas. And I thought it was sweet. Something for him and me to do together—to bring us closer. I liked learning about their lives. And when we met you, I was really happy for you to join us—I loved the idea of the three of us working together. But now I'm not so sure. I think it kind of became just Benjamin's thing. Not really something to share. And anyway, I probably never believed we'd really do it—I mean actually finish a whole opera and try to get it performed. Really it was just a way to be with each other."

"So you'll have to find a different way?"

"I guess so. Maybe." The door slowly closed behind us as we walked down the hall.

Later that week, Sarah and I went out for dinner so she could tell me about her dancing life. After dinner we walked back to my apartment for a cup of tea. Over dinner Sarah had described to me how in practicing Contact Improvisation they would start with just two dancers at a time, first standing close but not touching, each standing completely still, imagining tiny movements but not moving at all, then gradually, slowly, coming toward each other and finding each other's bodies. First with small movements, experimenting with small shifts of weight, then gradually leading to a bigger entwinement of bodies.

Although my apartment was tiny, when we walked in

I asked Sarah if she thought it might be possible for her to demonstrate for me how it worked—what she had described to me about Contact Improvisation. I moved the two chairs into the shower, one nestled in the other, and pushed the table to the corner. Then we stood in the middle of the small space, close together, facing each other but looking down at the floor.

I closed my eyes, and breathed slowly in and out, trying to feel each part of my body. We stood like that for a little while, and then Sarah interrupted the silence.

"Okay, now just the teensiest of movements, reach your hand toward me as slowly as you can imagine."

I felt the fingers of my right hand twitch into life, then my elbow awaken, my arm ever so slowly move forward, not knowing what I would find. My eyes were still closed. And just as I felt the barest sensation of my fingertip touching Sarah's soft skin—was it her arm? her neck?—I could feel at the same time her finger land on my cheek, ever so gently. I opened my eyes and looked up at her. Her beautiful face.

"Sarah?"

"Yes?"

"When you do this kind of dance, do you ever, I mean, you're probably not supposed to, but what if someone's touching you and, well, you know...what if..."

"What if?" She leaned toward me and our mouths found each other. And I thought, yes, what if, what if...

PART II

AND LOVE PROMISES MORE LOVE

HOW BABIES ARE MADE

Talking on the phone with Danny, our sperm donor and an old friend, I couldn't think straight. The hotel room had a hum. We were trying to make a plan, and it was an odd thing to do: not the way our fifth-grade teacher had taught us that babies were made. I felt I should be more comfortable—having known Danny for so long—and especially since he had been the donor once before when I myself had become pregnant with Tavi. Now it was Mandy's turn. Before we did my insemination, Mandy practiced filling a needleless syringe with a semen-like mixture of yogurt and water. I watched with pleasure the careful, precise movements of Mandy's hands as she stood over the sink, measuring, stirring, and carefully pulling up the plunger. Mandy was a materials scientist, and in a twist of synchronicity, her own work at the time had involved doing experiments on viscosity. She decided to read up on the viscosity of semen, so she could be sure her yogurt and water solution had the right consistency. It was really very interesting, the viscosity changes that semen went through; she became quite expert. At night sometimes she would read aloud to me.

"Hey, listen to this: 'researchers determined that a protein promoting increased viscosity evolves more rapidly in primate species with promiscuous females than in monogamous species. Sometimes the effects of this protein—semenogelin—are so strong that the semen becomes a solid plug in the vagina, preventing fertilization by the sperm of subsequent suitors.' This is fascinating."

It was fascinating to Mandy but I found the possibility horrifying.

Now on the phone with Danny, I could only refer to his part as doing his thing, as in, "We were thinking that after dinner you could just come over to the hotel room and do your thing while we took a little walk and then you could leave the jar and then we could come back and do our part."

So very awkward. I had better start getting more comfortable with the language. Doing his thing. Tavi was two now and soon we would have to explain all of this to her. I pictured Danny in fifth grade giving me little presents, the pieces of graphite that he managed to remove from his pencils. And now he was our sperm donor.

The hum was not driving Mandy crazy in the least, but after making arrangements with Danny, I thought perhaps I should try to find its source and eliminate it. Who knew? It could be some kind of very dangerous electro-magnetic thing. I put my ear next to the refrigerator. Loud, but not exactly the same quality of sound as the hum. I opened the door and observed that the freezer portion was swaddled in a thick layer of ice.

"This refrigerator needs defrosting," I said.

"Well, we're not going to defrost it now," said Mandy. She was sitting on one of two double beds with Tavi, reading her a book. Tavi leaned against Mandy's side, curling one finger around a lock of her thick brown hair, as she stared at the pictures. We had asked for a king-sized bed and had been given two doubles. I had already alienated the front desk clerk trying to argue our way into a different room, one with a king-sized bed. The hotel clerk had apologized, but there were simply no rooms with king-sized beds available. I had felt like Tavi, insisting on having applesauce when we had run out the day before and hadn't yet bought more.

"I certainly can't ask them for a new refrigerator, they hate me already." I turned the refrigerator dial to off. The room became much quieter.

"That's it," said Mandy. No. I could still hear the hum— could hear it even more loudly now that the refrigerator sound was gone.

"Don't you hear it?" I said.

Mandy cocked her head. "I hear a little something, but it's nothing. I don't even notice it." Mandy spoke in gentle even tones. I was incredulous. To me the sound of the hum was insidious, a steady pulsing sound I was sure would drive me crazy. I turned the refrigerator back on, walked over to the air conditioner, and after examining the panel of buttons, depressed the one for "quiet cool," eliciting a noise like a motorcycle revving up.

"That's a possibility," I said. "I might like to leave that on to mask the hum." Mandy looked up from the book.

"You would rather listen to that all night?"

"You wouldn't?"

"No, definitely not."

"Okay, okay, you're the one that needs to be comfortable. I defer to you." I shut the air conditioner off, and turned my head, listening. Next I walked over and put my ear up against the wall behind the bed where Mandy and Tavi were sitting. Loud, very loud. The wallpaper was scratchy.

"What's Mommy doing?" asked Tavi.

"Mommy thinks she hears a hum."

"Mommy does hear a hum," I said.

"What's a hum?"

"It's a kind of noise. An annoying pulsating noise. Do you hear it? Mmmm, mmmm, mmmm."

Tavi imitated my sound. "Mmmm, mmmm, mmmm."

"Hey, I think I've located the source of the hum," I tickled Tavi's stomach. Tavi shrieked and began to tickle me back.

"No—wait," I shouted. "I have an idea." I whispered into Tavi's ear. Tavi turned to Mandy and reached to tickle her under her arms.

"Try her feet," I coached. "Mama's feet are especially sensitive."

Mandy rolled gracefully to pull her feet out of Tavi's reach without kicking her. "Hey, no fair," she said. The three of us tumbled on the bed.

"Careful," I said. "Don't fall off." I lay back with my hands under my head and stared up at the stippled ceiling. "Now if we had a king-sized bed, I wouldn't have to worry about her falling off."

Once more I cocked my head. "Well I think this hum is coming through the walls. There may be no getting rid of it. We'll have to suffer."

"It's not bothering me," said Mandy.

"Good," I said. "That's the most important thing."

We met Danny and Ralph, Danny's partner, at my favorite Indian restaurant in the East Village. After dinner, Mandy discreetly handed Danny our room key so that he could do his thing in our room while she and I walked with Tavi over to Gramercy Park. As we approached the park, we could see little dots of light near the bushes.

"Hey, fireflies," said Mandy. She had been wanting to show Tavi fireflies and we hadn't seen any yet that summer.

"Lots of fireflies," I said.

"What are fireflies?" asked Tavi. Mandy pointed her finger.

"See the lights? Little flying insects are making those lights."

"I don't see," said Tavi.

I waved my arm in a sweeping motion across the front of the bush. "Just keep looking here and you'll see little lights flickering on and off, moving around."

Tavi trained her eye on the bush and waited. "I see, I see."

"Pretty neat, aren't they?" said Mandy. She squatted down to talk to Tavi, putting one hand gently on Tavi's back. "Do you know that fireflies have chemicals in their body that make them produce light? It's called bioluminescence."

"What's it for?" I asked.

"Well, it's a mating thing," said Mandy, standing up.

"What?" said Tavi.

"Mommy wanted to know why the fireflies make the

light. It's a way they have of talking to each other. One of them flashes the light and that means, 'I like you. Do you want to be friends? And another one flashes to say, 'Yes, let's be friends.'"

I reached for Mandy's hand and squeezed it. The three of us stood and watched the fireflies. I had a feeling I recognized from when I conceived Tavi, that somehow the universe knew what we were doing and was giving us a sign.

"It's a sign," I said softly to Mandy. "Tavi was water and this one will be fire."

Mandy laughed. "That's ridiculous."

"Look, how often do you see this many fireflies in New York? I'm sure it's a sign." And it was true, there were a lot of fireflies.

Danny had told us he would need about twenty minutes. We gave him twenty-five. We didn't want to walk in on him in the middle of something embarrassing. I was glad that Danny seemed pretty comfortable with all of this. When we got back to the hotel, the little jar was sitting on our night table. I brought Tavi into the bathroom to give her a bath. Tavi became interested in the double set of faucets in the bathtub. She insisted that I demonstrate that the upper faucets went with the shower, so I turned on the cold water, just for a second, but it sprayed me. "Ahhh," I shouted. Tavi laughed.

"Are you two okay in there?" Mandy yelled from the room.

"We're fine, are you okay?"

"Yes, fine, great." When the bath was over, Tavi ran into the room and climbed up onto the bed where Mandy was lying, knees up in the air. The jar was no longer on the night table.

"Airplane?" asked Tavi, leaning up against Mandy's feet. Mandy reached out for Tavi's hands, placed her feet solidly on Tavi's stomach, and straightened out her legs.

"I'm flying," said Tavi.

"Are you sure that's okay?" I asked, looking around to see where Mandy put the jar and the syringe.

"It's fine." Mandy steered Tavi gently down to the bed and kissed her on the forehead as she landed. I could imagine it: Tavi cuddled in close, and a baby asleep in the crook of Mandy's arm.

The hum that night was bad. In the middle of the night I decided that the noise from the refrigerator didn't mask the hum, it only magnified it. I knew it would be disastrous simply to turn off the refrigerator because all that ice would slowly melt and find its way onto the floor of the room. However, I also knew I had to do something to muffle the noise. I finally decided I would drag the refrigerator into the bathroom and close the bathroom door. The doors were solid in this hotel: that should help. And if there were any electro-magnetic waves, it would be safer with the refrigerator in another room. Mandy awoke as I was pulling the refrigerator across the floor.

"What are you doing?" she mumbled.

"It's the hum, I'm moving the refrigerator into the bathroom." It barely fit. I lay back down in bed next to Mandy. The noise was a little bit better, but still I heard the hum. I couldn't understand why it didn't disturb Mandy or Tavi. I hoped it wouldn't disturb the new little proto-person that might be forming right now inside

Mandy. All those sperm. Would the hum jar their concentration, prevent them from completing the task at hand? I was already feeling tenderly toward the sperm: maternal, protective. It would be different, not being the one who was pregnant. I felt protective of Mandy as well. Maybe Mandy didn't think the hum was bothering her, and maybe it wasn't, but I would watch out for her.

The call came from the midwife while we were all three playing together in Tavi's room. Mandy started to cry on the phone. She put her hand over the receiver and whispered to me: "Trisomy eighteen."

"What's the matter with Mama?" Tavi asked. "Why is Mama crying?"

"Mama just heard some very sad news. She'll tell you about it when she's ready to." All I could think of was: I must act normal for Tavi. I felt like ice.

Tavi was almost two and a half now. She rolled around on her green rug and said, "I'm a caterpillar." This was a game she liked, based loosely on the book *The Very Hungry Caterpillar*, in which she would pretend to munch on Mandy and me for a while, then she would lie still and we would roll her up in a sheet and say, "Now you're a chrysalis." When she found her way out, she would shout, "Now I'm a butterfly," and fly around the room. I could never understand why Tavi found this game so enjoyable, over and over again.

The book used the word "cocoon," but we were interested in maintaining some degree of scientific accuracy. Although the idea of a caterpillar eating through all those foods listed in the book—salami and cupcakes, for example—was absurd anyway. Why had we felt it was important to say "chrysalis" instead of "cocoon?" So many things seemed important until something really important happened. But how could you live thinking almost nothing mattered most of the time?

Now Mandy walked with the phone out of the room, and I had to say, "Oh no, don't eat me," and keep myself from crying, while Tavi munched away at me, searching my face with her big brown eyes. From the very first time I had nursed her, Tavi always seemed to be looking at me when she ate, taking in my face, as though she ate not only with her mouth but also with her eyes, even when she was only pretending to eat, as now. Our little caterpillar. And the other little caterpillar, what would become of that one, that we had already invested so much hope in? Tavi munched away and then flopped back on the rug. I wrapped Tavi up and kissed her forehead through the sheet. "Okay, you're a chrysalis." When Tavi flew out, she flew right out of the room and around our apartment, searching for Mandy, whom she found no longer on the phone but on our bed, crying.

Mandy couldn't stop crying and Tavi wanted to know why. I kept saying, "Mama feels sad, she heard some sad news." I rubbed Mandy's back, and then Tavi rubbed Mandy's back.

The day stretched out interminably until Tavi was in bed.

Because there was so much to talk about, we sat for a long time side-by-side on our bed, pillows propped up behind us, fingers interlocked, saying nothing. It was not a question of what to do. Neither of us had doubted for a moment, all that long day, that we would be in agreement about aborting the fetus. Still there was a lot to say. Finally, Mandy spoke.

"She said it's a girl."

Tears rolled down my cheeks. I could feel the hot wetness find a path down along my jaw and to my neck.

"I had this picture going in my head," I said. "Starting when we found out you were pregnant. Maybe even before. I would look at Tavi, whatever she might be doing, and I would imagine another daughter there with her. My girls. Like sometimes when I walked with Tavi down to the Kensington Market, I imagined myself walking with my two girls—each with a hand in mine—and we might be having a conversation, the three of us... It was so—I really tried not to get too invested in the two-girl thing, because it could have been a boy." I reached for a tissue. "Now I feel so stupid, like I was thinking on that level—boy, girl—when all along this other thing was the real level..." I turned and reached my hand out toward Mandy's abdomen. "Can I touch you?"

Mandy nodded, and then she began to cry as I gently rested my hand on her belly. "Are you afraid?"

"You mean about the abortion? Maybe a little afraid. But really I just want it out of me. I feel like my body's betrayed me," said Mandy.

"Your body? Your body's been wonderful. It's been doing this so beautifully."

"Beautifully? How can you say that, with this..."

"That's not your body. It's just bad luck."

"A bad egg."

"Or a bad sperm? Do they even know what causes it?"

"She said they don't know. The odds are one in three thousand."

I adjusted myself so that now my arm was around Mandy, and I held her close. "One in three thousand? Do you think it could have been that electro-magnetic thing in the hotel? That hum?"

Mandy laughed. "That's ridiculous." Then her laughter turned back into tears. She sobbed against my chest. "It's sad. It's just sad."

The next day we told Tavi.

"We found out that the baby growing inside Mama is very sick and can't grow anymore. It won't be able to be born. We're not going to have the new baby we hoped for." Tavi didn't quite understand the whole thing about babies being born. To her the bigger question was who had milk in her breasts. Once when Tavi had asked to nurse from Mandy, Mandy had said that her breasts had no milk. Tavi had asked why. Mandy had explained that a woman gets milk in her breasts when she grows a baby inside her body. Tavi knew she grew inside of me and therefore I was the one with the milk in her breasts. Now she said, "Maybe sometime I can grow inside of Mama, and then she will have milk in her breasts." As though the whole point of Mandy getting pregnant was so that she could be another source of milk for Tavi? "Well, Tavi," I said. "Once you're born, you're born. You will never grow inside of Mama."

A few days later, she said, "I know what happened. The baby died." I kept waiting for Tavi to ask how the dead baby would come out of Mama's body. But she never did.

The prenatal diagnostic clinic that had done the lab work referred us to an abortion clinic. The morning we were to go to the abortion clinic for the procedure,

Mandy's mother made an unexpected visit. The downstairs buzzer rang when we were busy getting Tavi dressed and ready to go to daycare. Although it was late October and fifty degrees out, Tavi wanted to wear shorts and a tank top. I peered out the window down to the sidewalk to see who was at the door.

"Mandy, it's your mother."

"My mother? What's *she* doing here?" She picked Tavi up and carried her in her arms down the stairs. She had been trying to hold Tavi as much as possible because once she had the abortion, she wouldn't be able to lift her for two weeks. I watched from the landing as Mandy opened the downstairs door.

"Want to see my room, grandma?" Tavi said. Grandma completely ignored Tavi, and barely said hello when I greeted her from the landing. Back upstairs, Tavi scrambled down from Mandy's arms and went into her room. "Grandma, want to see my new toys?"

Grandma stood in the hallway, her back to Tavi's room, groping for Mandy in an awkward hug, tears leaking out from dazed eyes. The family had never been skilled either at physical contact or at the expression of emotions. "Damn," she said. "Damn. My first grandchild."

"What's damn?" asked Tavi.

Mandy extracted herself from the embrace. "Mom, your first grandchild is Tavi."

"Well, but you know what I mean."

Too bad you can't abort your parents, I thought.

On the ride to the clinic, Mandy turned to me. "Where are you?" she asked. "What are you thinking about?"

"I was thinking about what your mother said this

morning," I said. "About this being her first grandchild."

"Oh, that was horrible. You don't think Tavi heard that, do you?"

"I don't think so. She probably wouldn't have understood it anyway."

"But if we ever do have another child..." said Mandy.

I reached for her hand and squeezed it. "I had this idea..." I explained my thought about aborting Mandy's mother.

Mandy gasped, but then she liked the idea very much. She was silent for a moment while thinking through the logical consequences of that idea.

"Of course we don't believe that abortion is murder," she finally said.

"Of course not. Nor do we believe in capital punishment, for that matter."

"Still, it might be pretty marketable." Mandy adjusted her seatbelt. "Maybe set up right next door to the prenatal diagnostic clinic: a parental diagnostic service."

I smiled. "Nice anagram."

"It could provide the same detailed analysis, confirmatory lab results, sober explanations, and referrals for the procedure. There could be counselors there and everything. They could hand out informative pamphlets."

"Right. That's perfect. And as soon as you say you were referred by parental diagnostics, they would assume it was some kind of problem and they would be all sympathy." We had stopped at a red light and I turned to Mandy.

"I was wondering," I said. "Do you think minors who wanted to abort their parents would have to have the consent of a babysitter? Or what?"

"Maybe a kindly teacher? Or a judge?"

"Probably every state would do it differently," I said.

"We're lucky to be living in Massachusetts," mused Mandy.

"I've always thought so."

There were three others in the waiting room, two men and a woman. The woman was already showing—maybe this wasn't her first pregnancy. She sat there in obvious distress, head turned toward the man sitting next to her, her face a question. He was reading a magazine. Another man sat on the couch across the room reading his Multivariable Calculus text. All three looked at us oddly as we hugged and kissed good-bye on the lips when Mandy was called to the back. "Love you, honey," I said and squeezed Mandy's hand one last time. I watched her cross the room and follow the nurse through a door.

Mandy and I had tried the night before to say some kind of a goodbye to this fetus, this possibility of a baby that never would be. Hard to do, trying at the same time not to think of it as something alive. So just what were we saying good-bye to? To possibility itself?

Four months later we were back in New York for two days. It was February this time, and a different hotel—on the west side, near Central Park. No hum. The first day, a Sunday, was beautiful: sunny and unseasonably warm. In the evening, while Mandy was busy inseminating in the hotel room, I walked over to Lincoln Center with Tavi, and we spent a long time together looking at the fountain, watching the water sparkle in the lights. The next day it was cold and cloudy and had begun to rain. The wind picked up. A storm was traveling up the coast from

Florida. It had spawned three tornadoes in Florida that destroyed a trailer park. Thirty-eight people died. Was that the omen? I didn't want to think about it. We went out to the Museum of Natural History, but after lunch returned to the hotel. All afternoon we waited for Danny to get out of work so we could do a second insemination and fly back to Boston. Tavi kept asking, "Can we go home?"

I said, "No, we have to wait a little longer. Our airplane doesn't leave until later."

"I want to go home," she would say.

"Soon," one of us would say.

The three of us sat on the bed. This time we had a king-sized bed. Tavi wanted us to tell her a story. "Tell me the story about when we went to New York."

"You mean the last time we went to New York? With the fireflies?"

"No, I want this time in New York."

"But it's still happening," said Mandy. "We're still in New York. How about if I tell you about the last time we went to New York?"

"I want to hear about this time."

Mandy couldn't do it. "We're in it," she kept saying. "We're still in it."

So I did it. I told about how we had decided it would be fun to go to New York and see Danny and Ralph again. At home we packed up and got ready to go to the airport, and then we drove to the airport and Mama parked the car while Tavi and I checked our luggage. Mama found us and we all went inside.

At that point I paused.

"And then I got a little upset," I told Tavi. Mandy reached for my hand and held it tight. I decided that it would be best to omit the next part of the story. That was the part where I became overcome with anxiety that our bags would not make it onto the plane, because we had checked them curbside.

"I got a little upset, but then I felt better. And we waited to get on the plane." I told the story of the plane ride and the taxi ride to the hotel and playing on the playground in Central Park: how funny it was that there were so many kids we had to wait in line for everything— a turn at the swings, and the slide, and the monkey bars, and the see-saw. I told about going out to dinner with Danny and Ralph, the walk to the fountain, sleeping in the big bed, breakfast, the museum, lunch, and running to make it back to the hotel before it started to rain.

"And then what?" asked Tavi.

"And now we're waiting until it's time to go to the airport. I think you and I will take a little walk soon, maybe just explore the hotel."

"With Mama?"

"No, just you and me."

"And then?"

"You want me to tell you a story about what hasn't happened yet, but is going to happen?" I asked.

"Yes, but a real story. Like what you just told. About our family."

"A real story about our family that hasn't happened yet?" I looked at Mandy. "She thinks I can predict the future."

Mandy squeezed my hand again. "Make it a good future," said Mandy. "Make it shine."

"You think whatever I tell, it will come true? Do you think it's safe to hope?" I asked Mandy. Tavi started to pick at the hem of the bedspread.

Mandy thought for a moment. "I think that imagining one's life may not be a sufficient condition for making the future come true, but it is absolutely a necessary one. And what did we come here for, if not to hope?"

"Well?" said Tavi. "The story?"

TIME SHARE

A week before our family left for a free weekend at the Royal Court Hotel, courtesy of Time Shares International, Lili announced at dinnertime, "I'm Carrie."

For quite a while, Lili's older sister Tavi had wanted Lili to be Carrie in a game based on the Laura Ingalls Wilder books. Carrie and her two sisters lived with their Ma and Pa a long time ago in the Big Woods of Wisconsin and then made their way to the Prairie.

Tavi was eight and she planned to be Mary, who was the oldest sister and could be quite bossy. Tavi liked the idea of telling Carrie what to do and even better, of telling Ma and Pa when Carrie did something wrong. Mandy and I would be Ma and Pa. But Lili always refused to play.

"This is great news!" I said. "Tavi, did you hear what Lili said? She's Carrie! We can finally play the Little House game and you can be Mary. You've been waiting for this."

"I don't want to be Mary anymore," said Tavi. Then she had an idea. "I'll be Spot." Spot was the cow.

"Now that Lili finally decides she wants to be Carrie,

you want to be Spot?"

Tavi shrugged her shoulders.

All week long, Lili insisted we call her Carrie, and she insisted on calling Mandy, 'Ma' and me, 'Pa.' I was already worried about the weekend, and this raised my anxiety a notch.

"What if she continues to call us Ma and Pa while we're at the hotel?" I asked Mandy.

"It'll be fine," said Mandy.

"And you told this place what our family looks like?"

"Yes. I was very explicit with them."

"It's just, we'll be bringing the kids into a situation where our family is obviously different from everyone else's. We don't know how people will react to us. There's a lot of hatred in the world. I don't want the kids to be hurt."

"I'm sure they'll be okay. It's not like they haven't encountered their share of stares and awkward questions... And the world needs to see families like ours. We'll be like ambassadors from the world of lesbian families to the straight world."

"And there's no obligation of any kind with the timeshare? You're sure?"

"For just two hours out of the whole weekend we'll listen to somebody's sales pitch, they'll give us a tour of a model unit, we'll watch a video. And that's it. The rest of the time we'll enjoy the hotel pool, even go to the beach, if it's not too cold. It'll be nice to be away. Just the four of us."

"A video? Our kids don't watch videos."

"A promotional video. You know, happy families testifying as to how great it is to have one of their time shares."

"Right, happy families just like ours. Ma, Pa, Carrie and Spot."

"Yeah, think of us as pioneers. With our cow."

As for Spot, she would frequently bump up against one or the other of us and begin to chew on our arm, apparently forgetting that cows were herbivores. Or she'd come up behind Carrie and break into a loud moo in order to startle her. On top of everything, was it possible that Spot was beginning to show the symptoms of mad cow disease?

We pulled the car up just beyond the entryway along a long circular driveway.

"Put your jackets on, girls, and get your backpacks. Here, let me help you." Mandy got out of the car and opened the back door to gather up the books and toys that lay scattered on the seat and the floor. A bellhop dressed in a red and gold uniform pushed a big cart toward us.

"Take your bags?" he offered. I opened the trunk for the bellhop while Mandy pulled our pillows out of the back seat of the car. We always traveled with our own pillows. The bellhop offered to put those on the cart as well. Mandy shrugged and handed them over to him. Our luggage looked odd, displayed on a baggage cart for everyone to see. We didn't have regular suitcases or hanging garment bags like other people; instead, we had several small, ragged backpacks, a canvas shopping bag filled with food for snacking, two brightly colored overstuffed duffel bags, an assortment of extra jackets and footwear and the four ungainly pillows.

We followed the cart into the lobby, where a big sign greeted us.

Tavi read: "Welcome Little Miss and Little Mister Warwick: Ballroom A. Welcome Church of God's Love: Green conference room. Welcome Greater Providence Chamber of Commerce, Workshop on Motivational Speaking: Ballroom B. Welcome guests of Coastal Resorts."

"They don't welcome us," said Tavi.

"Yes they do," said Mandy, pointing to the last item. "Here we are—the guests of Coastal Resorts."

"And who are Little Miss and Little Mister Warwick?" Tavi wondered.

Beyond the big sign, the hotel lobby was filled with children sporting pink "Little Miss Warwick" or blue "Little Mister Warwick" sashes, and pink or blue balloons.

"I think that's them," I gestured. "Looks like there are a lot of Little Miss and Mister Warwicks."

"Why are they here?" asked Tavi.

"They're here for a big contest," said Mandy.

"Are there prizes? Can we be in the contest too?" asked Tavi.

"I don't think so," I said.

"It's the kind of thing you have to register for in advance," said Mandy. Tavi seemed satisfied with the explanation.

"Can I have a balloon?" asked Lili.

"We'll have to ask," I replied vaguely.

"Check-in counter is this way," the bellhop pointed, "and I'll wait right here with your bags."

Along with the bellhop and our baggage cart, we

shared the elevator with a mother and her two children: a boy about six years old, dressed in a tuxedo and sneakers, and a girl about Lili's age in pink tights and a crinoline dress with multiple petticoats. Each sported a satin sash and a balloon. Lili stared at the balloons. Tavi stared at the little girl's outfit. The children's mother glanced at the baggage cart and then stared at Mandy and me. The bellhop stared straight ahead at the panel of floor numbers. Mandy looked down to avoid eye contact with anybody, and I discovered a mirror in the ceiling panel that allowed me to watch everyone. I felt unreal, as though we had mistakenly wandered onto the set of the wrong television show. Our show was being filmed in a different studio, but the cameras were rolling and the cast of this one, though annoyed, were trying their best to compose themselves in order to continue with their scene.

The elevator stopped to let out the mother with her two little Warwicks. "Wow," said Lili as we watched the boy glide down the hallway. We had never before seen sneakers with wheels embedded in the soles. The elevator door closed.

"I don't get it," said Tavi. "Are they all Little Mister and Little Miss Warwick? They all seem to have those sashes and balloons. If it's a contest, shouldn't there be just one winner?"

"Maybe all the contestants get a sash and a balloon, just for being contestants. But the actual winner gets something else," I speculated.

"I want a balloon," said Lili. The elevator stopped at our floor.

We liked the room. It had some kind of silvery,

textured wallpaper and a couple of big prints covered in glass with stock scenes of the ocean: a sailboat in one, a sunset in the other. Over one of the beds hung a smaller print of children playing on the beach with pails and shovels.

I sprawled out on the bed and pointed to the beach picture. "Looks like fun," I said to Tavi.

"I am not going to the beach in March," Tavi said. "Can we go to the pool?"

Tavi and Lili opened every drawer and every door and tried out the beds.

Meanwhile, Mandy started to unpack. I loved to watch Mandy's hands. They moved like a dance, unzipped the bag, opened the flap, pulled out a stack of shirts, separated them into two neat piles at the edge of the bed: clothes for Lili, clothes for Tavi.

"Come, Tavi, Lili, put your clothes away, and I'll take you to the pool," Mandy said.

"I'm not Lili, I'm Carrie."

"Okay, Carrie," said Mandy. She handed Lili her pile of clothes and pointed to the drawer. "Let's check out the pool."

"Do we need our bathing suits?" asked Lili.

"No, we'll just go scout it out first, figure out how it works." She ushered them out the door.

I was tired. I could have dozed off a little right then, but since Mandy had done all the unpacking *and* taken the girls down to the pool, I thought I should do something useful. I looked around. A T.V. guide lay on top of the television cabinet. I retrieved it and sprawled back onto the bed. We did not have a television at home, because of its known ill-effects on young children, but if I could find something palatable to watch after dinner, it might be a special treat for Lili and Tavi. Just this one time. Now I had a sense of purpose.

When Mandy and the kids came back from the pool they were bursting with news. "A special thing's going to happen at the pool tomorrow morning!" Tavi shouted.

"What kind of special thing?" I asked.

"People getting dunked."

"What? What do you mean? Witch trials?" I looked at Mandy.

"Christian people," said Tavi.

Mandy explained, "You know that Church of God's Love group that's meeting in the green conference room?" I was always impressed with Mandy's ability to retain the salient facts. "They're going to use the pool to do baptisms."

"And we can watch!" shouted Tavi.

I gave Mandy a look. "We can watch? Do we want to watch?"

"Tavi wanted to watch. She thought it would be interesting."

Lili was getting a certain look on her face that suggested a question was on its way. I waited for her to speak. "Are they going to push me in the pool? I don't want to get water in my eyes." Tavi grabbed Lili's shoulders and pretended to push her into the water.

"No, no, I don't want to," screamed Lili.

"Tavi, please," I said. "It's okay, Lili. We're Jewish. Jews don't get baptized, don't worry."

"But we get mikvahs," said Tavi.

"What's a mikvah?" asked Lili.

"I don't really know," said Tavi. "But Ruthie told me

she had to have one when she was four so that she could be Jewish, and they pushed her in the water."

"Will they do that to me?" asked Lili.

"I don't think so," said Tavi. "They didn't do it to me."

I sat up. "The mikvah is like a special bath. It's a Jewish ritual of purification that some religious Jews do at certain times. But you don't have to worry about it. We are secular Jews. Nobody is going to push either of you into the water unless you say it's okay. All right?"

"Mama's not Jewish. Mama's nothing," said Tavi.

"Then she's safe. We can all relax," I said. I threw the T.V. guide over to Tavi. "Look what's in here. On page seven."

"What, what is it?" Tavi had never seen a T.V. guide before.

I leaned over, opened the guide, found the page and pointed to it. "The World Championships. After dinner tonight. Downhill skiing and figure skating. On television."

"Wow, television. Mommy's really letting her hair down," said Mandy.

Tavi and Lili looked puzzled. "Mommy doesn't have enough hair to let it down," said Tavi.

I tugged at my very short, graying hair.

"It's just an expression," said Mandy. "I meant—Mommy's feeling relaxed about things." The girls stared at Mandy, and then at me, not quite sure what Mandy was talking about.

After dinner that night we went back to our room to watch the World Championships. Tavi and Lili put on their pajamas and brushed their teeth. The show opened with an edited sequence of shots from the preliminary trials. Over and over skiers fell and slid down the hill in multiple somersaults, crashing into gates along the way.

"I don't like this," said Tavi, putting her hands over her eyes. "Turn it off."

"Turn it off," cried Lili. Mandy turned off the television.

"Mommy, why did you think we would like that television?" asked Tavi.

"I just... I didn't..." I didn't know what to say.

Later that night after the kids were asleep, I handed Mandy an envelope. "Did you see this?"

Mandy turned the envelope over. "Dr. and Mrs. Mandy Lyons and family. What is this?"

"It's the information from Coastal Resorts. They gave it to us when we checked in."

"Dr. and Mrs.? I told them on the phone we were two women. Partners. Not married. I gave them your name."

"Either they weren't paying attention or their computer couldn't handle it."

"I specifically asked them if they would be comfortable with a two-mother family."

I took the envelope from Mandy's hand and opened it. "'Dear Dr. and Mrs. Mandy Lyons: We hope you enjoy your complimentary stay at the Royal Court Hotel... blah blah.... We look forward to meeting you on Saturday at 2 pm for the two-hour informational program about our time-shares... blah blah.... Coastal Resorts offers the finest facilities and recreational opportunities for the whole family.... Moms, Dads, and children of all ages will find everything they're looking for in a vacation resort. Etc. etc.'" I looked up at Mandy. "My guess is Coastal Resorts doesn't completely understand the profile of our family. What if they become hostile in front of the kids?"

"Don't worry, we'll talk to them in the morning. I'm sure it'll be fine. And really, the worst that can happen is they won't want us on the tour. So we'll have gotten a free night in a hotel without having to do a thing."

"Right, a free night with all the little pink and blue Warwicks and the born-agains."

"Naomi, this is the world. We can't keep our children from knowing about all the things in the world we might disagree with or perceive as dangerous. We wouldn't want to."

"I just don't want them to get hurt."

"Everyone gets hurt. What we want is to help them to be resilient."

"Right, resilient. Like wax on a floor tile." I knew Mandy was right, but still I felt wary.

On Saturday morning we all went down to the pool in our bathing suits and beach robes. The baptisms were supposed to begin at 9, and when we got there at 8:30 several members of the hotel staff were busy setting up folding chairs around the pool. Tavi walked over to the edge of the pool and dipped her toe in. "It's cold."

"If it were me, I would want to be baptized in the Jacuzzi," I said. We dumped our towels on a couple of lounge chairs and dragged the chairs into position, close enough for a good view, but maintaining a discreet distance from the group of worshippers, who had begun to file into the pool area and were taking their seats around the pool.

A white man dressed in a white suit stood near the steps at the shallow end, holding a cordless microphone. He was wearing bright red rubber water shoes that seemed incongruous with his outfit. A line of people stood near him at the top of the steps.

"O Lord, my soul shall live with thee," he began to speak. "Do thou give my spirit rest."

Tavi asked, "Is he the priest?"

Mandy answered her, "Something like that. I think we'd call him a minister or a preacher."

I leaned over to whisper to Mandy. "If he drops that microphone into the pool, will he be electrocuted, or will the rubber shoes save him?" Mandy was a scientist and I always relied on her expertise in such matters. She gave me a look. "Shhh. Be respectful."

"What?" said Tavi.

"Restore me and give me life," he continued. "Bitterness had indeed been my lot in place of prosperity. But thou by thy love hast brought me back from the pit of destruction; for thou hast cast all my sins behind thee." The first woman, a tall honey-blonde in a white dress and pink rubber water-shoes, stepped up closer to him. He took her hand and together they walked down two steps so that the water was at knee-level. I turned to look at Tavi and Lili. They were both riveted, staring at the man and the woman. I wondered what they were thinking.

"Speak with me," the man said to the woman. And together they spoke: "The Lord is at hand to save me; so let us sound the music of our praises all our life long in the house of the Lord." At this point the man handed the microphone to his assistant, put one arm around the woman's shoulders and another around her waist, and tipped her backwards so that her head and her whole body were briefly submerged in the water.

"She has clothes on!" Lili shouted. "Her clothes are

getting all wet!" Lili and Tavi giggled.

There were about ten people in all. By the fourth one, Tavi was mouthing the words along with them. "The Lord is at hand to save me; so let us sound the music of our praises all our life long in the house of the Lord." By the sixth, she was grabbing onto Lili and pretending to dunk her backwards into the lounge chair. The last person was a pale woman with glasses and long dark hair, and a rather pinched face. She handed her glasses to the honey-blonde who had gone first. The blonde woman squeezed her hand. This woman looked very scared. When the preacher started to say, "Bitterness had indeed been my lot in place of prosperity. But thou by thy love hast brought me back from the pit of destruction; for thou hast cast all my sins behind thee," she closed her eyes tight.

"I wonder what those sins were," I whispered to Mandy. When the woman emerged from the water, her face seemed transformed, as though someone had snipped the thread that had been holding it tight.

That was the end. The ones who had been watching all got up from their folding chairs and everybody was hugging everybody else. Tavi grabbed Lili's arm and started pulling her toward the pool. "The Lord is at hand to save you."

"I don't want to be saved," screamed Lili. "I don't want to be saved. I don't want to get my eyes wet."

Mandy turned to me. "Are you coming in the water?" I was still watching the group of worshippers as they left the pool area, wondering what they were thinking, imagining what their lives were like. Tavi stomped back over to Mandy and me.

"Lili won't play with me. She doesn't want me to dunk

her and I told her she could dunk me and she said she just wants to be Carrie. She hates me." I pulled Tavi onto my lap.

"Bitterness has indeed been your lot, but the Lord is at hand to save you. Do you want to be saved? Sound the music of your praises." I started to tickle Tavi, who squirmed and shouted, "Save me, save me."

I turned to Mandy. "I think I have to save this girl. Can you handle Carrie?"

"Carrie is beyond saving," said Mandy.

We all made our way over to the pool steps. "Speak with me," I said to Tavi, as I led her by the hand down to the bottom step. But before I could say another word, Tavi pulled her hand out of mine and pushed me down under the water.

"So let us sound the music of our praises," shouted Tavi. "You're saved!"

At lunch, we stood for a long time at the buffet bar trying to decide what to put on our plates. Two women came up behind us.

"Oh, excuse us," said Mandy. "Why don't you go on ahead."

One of them, a tall blonde, leaned toward Lili, "Hello, there." Lili hid behind Tavi.

The blonde looked at Tavi. "Have you been having fun at this hotel?" she asked.

"Yes, we went swimming. And we saw you in the pool. At the baptism."

"Did you? What did you think of that?"

"I liked it," said Tavi. "It looked like fun."

At this the other woman laughed. "I was so scared,"

she said, "I don't know how to swim and I thought for sure I was going to drown." We adults exchanged friendly smiles. Tavi and Lili returned to the task of choosing their food and then carried their trays over to a table.

While we were eating, a group of children with balloons attached to their wrists lined up at the buffet. "I want a balloon," said Lili.

"You know, those are helium balloons," I said. "Which is what makes them stay up. There's helium in them and helium is lighter than air, which means if you're holding one of those balloons outside and you accidentally let go, then the balloon floats away. And not only do you lose the balloon, but it floats out over the ocean, and when the helium starts to leak out of the balloon, the balloon sinks down to the ocean. Then a duck might see the balloon, and think it's something to eat. It scoops it up to eat it, but the balloon is not good to eat, and it makes the duck very very sick, and then the duck might even die. So those balloons are not a good thing."

"I'm done," said Lili.

"Did you have to say that to her?" asked Mandy.

"I'm sorry," I said. "I'm sorry, Lili. I just don't think we can get one of those balloons. They're for the Little Miss and Mr. Warwicks. I'm really sorry."

"What are we doing after lunch?" asked Tavi.

"We have to meet with some people so they can tell us about a place to stay by the ocean."

"I don't want a different place. I like this hotel," said Lili.

"We wouldn't stay there now. They just want to tell us about it and show it to us."

"It sounds boring," said Tavi.

"Well, we'll bring some books and toys for you. It'll be okay. We get to go for a ride in a little bus," said Mandy.

"And remember," I whispered to Mandy as we cleared our trays from the table. "When we're at this thing—just don't sign anything. No matter what it is, no matter what they say, don't sign anything."

"Can you relax?" she asked. "It's all going to be fine."

A woman in a navy-blue tailored suit holding a clipboard greeted us with an outstretched hand and a big smile at the entrance to one of the small hospitality rooms off the hotel lobby. "Hello, come on in. I'm Jackie."

"I'm Mandy," said Mandy, as she shook Jackie's hand.

Jackie looked confused as she scanned the paper on her clipboard. "And you've brought your sister?"

"No, this is my partner, Naomi. And our children."

I offered my hand to Jackie, whose smile, if somewhat diminished, remained committed to her face.

"I have you down here as Dr. and Mrs. Mandy Lyons. Maybe there's been some mistake?"

"Mama's not a doctor!" said Tavi.

Jackie dropped the smile. "Perhaps we should start by verifying your personal information. You did speak to one of our phone representatives? She must have entered it incorrectly."

The room was furnished with a large veneer desk and a couple of comfortable armchairs upholstered in a red-flowered fabric that matched the carpeting. Jackie sat behind the desk and motioned for Mandy and me to sit on the chairs. Tavi and Lili each climbed onto a lap.

"It isn't Dr. Mandy Lyons?"

"Well, actually I *am* a doctor—although not a medical

doctor," Mandy apologized.

"And it's Naomi...?"

"Yes."

"And these are your children?"

"Yes. *Our* children," I said, pointing to Mandy and myself, just in case she hadn't understood. She seemed unfazed.

After Jackie determined that the rest of the information was accurate, she put down her clipboard, once again smiled broadly, and launched into her spiel. She explained we'd be taking a shuttle bus with a few other prospective owners to see the furnished model apartment, where we'd also have the opportunity to watch a short informational video and ask questions. Then we'd return to the hotel where she'd meet with us individually again. For now, she just wanted to emphasize that we were fortunate to be eligible for the pre-construction price, at a great discount from what it would cost once all the condos were completed. "Any questions at this point?"

"Do we have to wear seatbelts on the bus?" asked Tavi.

"Nobody has ever asked me that question," said Jackie. "I'm afraid I don't know."

The shuttle bus had seats that faced inward all around the interior perimeter and no seatbelts. Tavi and Lili sat on their knees so we could look out the window, with Mandy's and my hands at the ready behind their backs in case the bus should come to a sudden stop. The Stevens family and the Porter family joined us. The Stevens family was big-boned and blonde-haired: Mom, Dad, two boys about eight and ten, and a girl about four. The Porter family was pale-skinned, dark-haired and thin, with two boys about six and eight. The mother wore black leather knee-high boots over tight jeans and a thick sweater that reached to her thighs. She used the window as a mirror to check her hair and lipstick. The father sat with one boy on either side, an arm across their shoulders. The bus driver had a microphone and spoke as he drove us to the apartment, describing the local attractions.

Tavi and Lili made themselves right at home in the model apartment, although they stayed clear of the living room, where a promotional video was playing on the television. They spent a long time playing on the bunk bed but decided that for sleeping they would use the bedroom with the two twin beds. Lili especially liked the pink lamp on the bedside table in that room. They had some disagreement about who should have which bed. We left them in there to figure it out while we checked out the master bedroom suite.

"How's the mattress?" I asked as Mandy sat down on the queen bed.

Mandy bounced up and down a bit. "Seems pretty good."

I lay down on the other side. "Not bad. What time is it, anyway? How long are we supposed to stay here?" I didn't wear a watch, so I reached for Mandy's arm and held it steady with two hands as I read hers.

At that moment Mr. Porter wandered into the room, preceded by his two sons. He glanced at the bed, said a quick "Excuse me," and grabbed his boys by their shirts. "C'mon, boys," he said, making a hasty retreat.

We both burst out laughing. "Whoops," said Mandy.

"Poor guy, he looked so embarrassed. Two women on the bed! What do you think he'll tell his sons?"

We returned to the open living room/dining room to check out the video. But I found it difficult to pay attention to the screen, distracted by the thought of owning the very same apartment as either one of these two families. What if we had the two weeks immediately following the Porters? Would there be hair products left behind in the shower? I was sure Mr. Porter wouldn't be happy about sharing a bedroom with Mandy and me.

Back at the hotel we endured an hour of hard sell by Jackie. She explained all about the other resorts we would have access to if we bought two weeks a year at this one. Trades, exchanges, bi-yearly four-week plans, points for off-season weeks, two for threes: I imagined the concept meetings in which people had actually hashed out all these various schemes. And then it was over.

"We're done! We did it!" I cheered as I shut the door to our room. "Now it's just our family for the rest of the weekend! We can relax! Hurray!"

We were not quite done. At three a.m., Mandy and I were awakened when the fire alarm went off in our room. I tried calling the front desk to find out what was happening, while Mandy gathered a few of our things together. "Busy tone. Busy busy busy," I said. "Let's just get out of here." I scooped Lili up, while Mandy gently woke Tavi up and ushered her out into the hallway, putting her own hands over Tavi's ears.

Others were already in the hallway. Mandy once read an article about how most people who survived plane crashes had made it a point to locate the exits in advance and plan an escape route. She had quietly gotten in the habit of doing that herself, not only when we were in airplanes, but also in hotels and theaters and other indoor public spaces. When we left our room, Mandy, therefore, knew just where to go, and something about her certitude seemed to attract the other people, because as we walked down the hallway toward the exit door others fell in line, so that we became the leaders of a strange procession of adults and children in pajamas, bathrobes, nightgowns, sweat suits, and other more unusual forms of nightdress, some holding two hands up over their ears, a few children holding Little Miss or Little Mister Warwick balloons, walking down the hallway toward the emergency exit. When we had almost reached the exit a hotel clerk in uniform popped out of the stairwell and put her hand up. We all stopped to look at her.

"It's okay," she shouted, or tried to shout over the noise of the fire alarm, "It was just a smoking toaster. There isn't any fire. You can take the elevator down to the lobby, where it's quieter. We have to wait for the fire department to turn off the alarm system." Only the people closest to her could hear her, so an odd game of "telephone" ensued, in which a few at a time people nodded their heads, shouted the message on to the next group, and turned to walk toward the elevator.

The lobby was quieter, although not exactly quiet. Outside the big glass windows we could see three fire engines with lights flashing.

"Can we go swimming?" Tavi asked.

"Tavi, honey, it's three o'clock in the morning," said Mandy.

"But we're up. And you'd think a pool would be a good place to be if there's a fire. Because it's filled with water.

So we'd be safe."

"It's good logic," I said. "Safe and saved."

Mandy sighed. "There is no fire. We're just waiting for the firefighters to turn off the alarm and then we can go back up to our rooms and go to sleep. Anyway, the pool is closed."

"Aww," said Tavi.

"Maybe you and Lili would like to get a closer look at the fire engines," suggested Mandy. "Want to walk over with me? What about you, Lili?"

But Lili had her own project going, trying to find a comfortable position in my arms. So Mandy and Tavi walked over to the front windows while I found a place to sit on one of the sofas. Lili kept rearranging herself on my lap, all the while holding my hands over her ears. She was trying to tuck her head in against my chest but had to negotiate around the zipper of my fleece anorak. No matter where she landed, it was not right. When Mandy and Tavi walked back over to us I pointed with my chin to Lili and said, "I can't tell you how uncomfortable and annoying this is."

"Do you want me to take a turn holding her?"

"Oh, no, I think we're close, she's settling in," and indeed Lili had finally seemed to find a stable position, when Tavi said, "Look at that pink woman," and Lili sat bolt upright.

"Which?" she said. Pink was Lili's favorite color. Tavi pointed discreetly at two women who were walking toward us. The dark-haired one was wearing fluffy pink slippers, pink pajamas, and a pink robe, and she was clutching a pink elephant in her hand.

"Hey, it's those women from the baptism," said Tavi.

The women seemed to be heading right for the sofa. "The Lord is at hand to save you," said Tavi to Lili.

"Is it okay if we sit down here?" asked the honey blonde, wearing some kind of gauzy apricot-colored sleep set.

"Of course," said Mandy, scooting closer to me, and pulling Tavi in next to her. "There's plenty of room." The two women sat down.

"Isn't this just terrible," the gauzy woman said, but she was smiling. "And these poor children having to be up in the middle of the night. Aren't they just darling?"

The unusual intimacy of the situation seemed to call for introductions. "My name is Rhonda," said the gauzy blonde.

"I'm Mandy."

"Sue Ann," said the pink one.

"Naomi."

Rhonda leaned toward Lili, "And what's your name?" Lili tucked her head back into my chest.

"That's Lili," said Tavi. "She's my sister." Lili reached her foot out to nudge Tavi. "And I'm Tavi." Lili nudged Tavi again. "What is it?" Tavi leaned over Mandy to get closer to Lili. Lili whispered something into Tavi's ear. "Oh," she said, turning back to Rhonda and Sue Ann. "She wants me to tell you she's not Lili, she's Carrie. It's a game we play. From the Little House books. I like to be Mary. And Mama's Ma," she pointed to Mandy, "and Mommy's Pa." I smiled and put my arm around Mandy, as though someone was taking a family portrait. "Sometimes I'm Spot," Tavi went on, "Spot is a cow."

At that moment the alarm stopped sounding.

"Praise the Lord," said Rhonda.

"Bedtime," said Mandy. We all got up and started walking toward the elevators. On our way over we passed a table filled with brochures describing local attractions. Tavi stopped.

"Hey, cool, look. Can we take some of these?"

Lili slid out of my arms. "Me too?" she asked. I hung back with Lili and Tavi to look at the display, while Mandy continued walking with Rhonda and Sue Ann over to the elevators.

Later, lying in bed, after Tavi and Lili had fallen asleep again, I whispered to Mandy, "Those women were kind of a trip. That pink outfit. And the elephant. I kind of liked them. And then Tavi going on about you being Ma and me being Pa. I'm almost sorry they didn't have a chance to respond. I wonder what they thought about us."

"Do you know what Rhonda asked me when we were walking over to the elevators? She wanted to know if she could pray for Lili."

"What? What did you say?"

"I just said thank you."

"You what? You said she could pray for Lili? Does she know Lili's Jewish? Why would she want to pray for Lili? What did she mean? What kind of prayers? We don't believe in that kind of thing," I said.

"I have no idea what she meant. I thought she was just trying to be nice, so I said thank you."

"Do you think she thinks something is wrong with Lili? Do you think it was because we're lesbians? What if she starts praying for Lili, and it has some weird effect on her?"

"If you don't believe in it, why would you think it could hurt her? Who cares if she prays for Lili? You yourself said you kind of liked them," said Mandy.

"I liked them before I knew she was going to prey on Lili."

"Pray *for* Lili," said Mandy. "But I really don't think it has anything to do with Lili. I just think it's something that she does for herself, that makes her happy. I think in her mind it's a friendly thing to do."

"What do you think she would pray? What exactly did she say?"

"What she said was, 'Your little girl is such an angel. Could I pray for her?'"

"I don't get it," I said. "There are hundreds of little Miss and Misters roaming around this hotel, any one of whom clearly needs someone to pray for them, actually desperately needs some kind of divine intervention in their lives, and she wants to pray for Lili. It simply makes no sense."

Lili awoke bright and early the next morning and climbed into bed with Mandy and me, ready to play. I looked her over carefully. "Do you feel okay? Are you all right?" Lili nodded. The brochures she and Tavi had picked up from the hotel lobby were in a stack on the night table near Mandy. Mandy reached for them and handed them to Lili. "Here," she whispered. "Why don't you look at these?"

While Mandy and I tried to get a little more sleep, Lili sat between us, pointing to the pictures and saying, "I'm her... no, I'm her."

"Shhh," Mandy said softly. "You'll wake Tavi up. Tavi needs her sleep."

Lili glanced longingly at the sleeping Tavi. She really

wished Tavi were awake so they could play this game together. "Sorry," she said, rather loudly. "I didn't mean to wake Tavi." Tavi rolled over dramatically. She stretched, fluttered her eyelids, and sighed.

"I think Tavi's awake," said Lili. She leaned over Mandy to get a better look at Tavi, and Mandy shouted, "Ow, ow, your elbow." Lili leaned back again. "Sorry," she said. Tavi sat up abruptly.

"Can we go to the pool?" she asked.

I sat up too, glanced down at the brochures Lili had been playing with, and picked one up. "Hey, this looks good, this is exactly where I think we should go today. Listen. 'The National Wildlife Refuge: a vast diversity of habitats from salt and freshwater marshes, to grasslands, to sandy beaches and dunes. Three miles of trails wind their way through upland areas and along the rocky shore. The refuge is a great place to watch wildlife with over 200 bird species present seasonally including harlequin ducks, scoters, and eiders.'"

"Will the ducks be dead from the balloons?" asked Lili.

"The ducks will be fine," I said.

"I really wanted to swim in the pool again," said Tavi.

"We can do both," I said. "Pool first, then ocean."

"You know, I had a dream last night," said Tavi. "In my dream, you made us go to the ocean even though I didn't want to, and we were playing that game where you stand close to the water, and when the waves come you try to run away from them, and then Lili fell when we were running and a big wave came and splashed all over her and carried her into the ocean and she drowned."

"That hurts my feelings," said Lili.

"Well, I can't help it, that was the dream."

After swimming one last time in the pool, we checked out of the hotel and drove to the National Wildlife Refuge. It was a bright, sunny day, and even near the ocean it was not too windy. The coastline was rocky, with some sandy patches, too. We had intended to look for seals and harlequin ducks, but in fact what Tavi and Lili spotted when we approached the water's edge was an opening in the rocks that was just wide enough to fit through. On the other side of the narrow opening, the rocks curved around to shelter a small part of the beach, the size of a little room.

"I know what we could do," said Tavi. "I have a great idea. We could pretend this is our house. We could play Little House in the Big Woods. We could be Mary and Carrie and Ma and Pa."

"Great idea!" said Mandy. "Let's do it."

"It could be the Little House by the Ocean," I said.

Tavi frowned. "But they were nowhere near the ocean."

"Maybe the ocean could be a great lake." I offered. "Little House by the Great Lake."

Mandy and Lili had begun to collect seaweed and shells and stones.

"Wait, don't start without me," said Tavi.

"Well, Mary dear, we certainly could use your help," said Mandy. I stood looking at the ocean.

"You know, Caroline," I said (Ma was Caroline, and Pa, Charles), "I believe that when the tide comes in, this little house will not only be *by* the Great Lake, it will be *in* the Great Lake."

"Lakes don't have tides," said Mandy.

"Very funny," I said. "I mean it. I think it's low tide and

when it comes in it will go all the way past those rocks."

"Let's cross that bridge when we come to it, Charles dear," said Mandy.

I thought for a minute. "Maybe I'll go see if I can catch some fish for supper," I said. "If that's okay with you, Caroline?"

"That's fine, Charles. Take your time. I'll be okay here with the girls."

"But I want you to play with us, too," said Tavi.

"Mary, we have to eat. I must try to catch some fish. You stay here and help Ma with the chores, and keep an eye on Carrie, will you? I'll be back soon."

I set out. The tide was still low enough for me to walk along the sand, near the water's edge. I scanned the ocean with my binoculars. I could see a group of harlequin ducks, not too far out. There were perhaps twenty or thirty of them, some floating, some bobbing their heads under and wiggling their tails up in the air, performing their own kind of baptismal ritual. One mother duck with a line of five ducklings behind her swam closer to the shore. I was reminded of something I had once read: that when a mother duck feels safe, she will lead the way and let her ducklings follow, but if she senses danger, she makes sure all her ducklings are in front of her, so she can keep an eye on them.

I kept watching to see if she would change their configuration, but apparently no dangers threatened, since she continued to stay in front to lead her ducklings in a meandering path. I resumed walking along the water's edge until the sandy shoreline turned to rock. I climbed up the boulders to look for a flat place to sit. Leaning back, closing my eyes, I soaked up the warmth of the sun on my face and listened to the waves and the screeching sounds of the seagulls.

I thought about being Pa. When I was young, playing house with my two sisters, I always ended up in the role of the father. Rachel was the mother, and Leah was the daughter. That's just how it was. Sometimes I wanted to be the mother, but I never asked for that, because I thought my sisters would laugh at me. There was some way in which I knew I was different from other girls and that meant I couldn't be the mother. Wouldn't ever be a mother. The desire to actually be a mother, to have children of my own, was something I never spoke about to anybody, during all the painful years of high school and college. I believed it could never happen. And now—look at how my life turned out.

I stood up. From up on the rocks I could see my family, three little dots, and I lifted my binoculars to get a better look. I focused on each one in turn. Lili had a pile of shells and a pile of stones and was carefully lining up the shells and placing a stone in each one. I moved my head a bit to find Tavi, who was busy doing something with seaweed over near Mandy. I could see that Tavi was talking, maybe explaining something to Mandy; it was clear that whatever she was doing with the seaweed was secondary to the conversation. And then I shifted the binoculars so that Mandy was in full view, braiding some strands of seaweed with her fingers while she listened to Tavi—nodding, looking interested, occasionally glancing back to where Lili was sorting her shells and stones. My girls. My three girls. My family.

I scampered down the rocks and hurried back.

When I got back to the little house, Tavi and Lili came running over to greet me. "Pa, you're back."

"You see, Mary," said Ma as she walked over toward us. "I told you Pa would come back."

"I hope you weren't worried about me, Caroline."

"Oh no, Charles, we were fine."

"Well I had quite an adventure."

"Tell us the story, Pa," said Mary.

"Maybe Pa is ready for supper."

"Yes, let's eat first, and then I'll tell you my story." There was an elaborate meal set out, of stones and shells and seaweed and feathers. Before we ate, Mary and Carrie insisted that I guess what everything was supposed to be, which took longer than the eating of it. Then I told my story.

Pa and the Whales

"I intended to catch us some good fish, so I walked down to a spot where I saw a lot of gulls feeding. I was having no luck with the fish, and then I thought I heard a little sea lion or dolphin in the ocean calling for help, so even though I knew the tide was coming in, I walked all the way out on a big sandbar, but when I got to the edge of the water I saw nothing, only some seals playing happily in the water."

"Were there little seals and big seals?" asked Lili.

"Why yes, there were four seals, two big mom seals and a medium-sized seal, and a little seal."

170

"That was me, I was the little seal," said Lili.

"I was the medium one," said Tavi.

"Well, to continue, when I started walking back, I saw the sand bar had gotten cut off, so I couldn't get back to the beach. I didn't know what I would do. The water got closer and closer on both sides, and soon I was standing on just a tiny patch of sand the size of one shoe, and then even that was gone, and the water was getting higher, and then it was over my head, and I tried to swim to shore, but the strong current was taking me out further into the ocean. I thought I would drown. Just then, a big whale came along as though it knew I was in trouble. Actually it was three whales, one big, one medium, one small. The small one swam right up close to me, and I managed to climb up onto her back. Then the medium-sized whale came up close to us, and from the back of the small one I managed to climb onto the medium one. And in turn the big one came up close and I climbed onto her back. Like climbing up three stairs. And then the big whale carried me close to the shore. The smaller whales accompanied us. So I was safe, and I walked back home to you. But I caught no fish."

"Well, Charles, you know what I like to say: 'All's well that ends well,'" said Mandy.

"The smallest one saved you?" asked Lili.

"They all did," I said. "The three of them together."

"Why didn't you just stay on the smallest one?" asked Tavi.

"I needed all three of them to save me."

"Your clothes aren't wet," said Tavi.

As we spoke, the waves were clearly coming closer to our little house. Mandy said, "Mary, Carrie, I think we should climb up on these rocks. The tide really is coming in."

"But this is our house," said Lili. "I want to keep playing."

"It's time for us to leave now, anyway, Lili. We have to be getting home."

"I want to stay in the house."

"Caroline, I'm afraid the fishing is just not good enough anymore in these parts. We're going to have to move," I said.

"Oh, Charles. And I was hoping the girls would be able to go to school here."

"We don't care, do we, Carrie? We want to move," said Tavi.

Lili looked uncertain. I pulled a couple of tissues from my pocket. "Here girls. Take these cloths and wrap up a few of your most precious belongings. But hurry. The horses are waiting."

Tavi and Lili each picked out a few of the stones and shells. Then the four of us stood at the edge of the water. We had to dip our hands in to see just how cold it was. The foam surf brushed against the edges of our boots as we bent down and let the water kiss our fingertips. It was extremely cold.

Saved, I thought. *I've been saved. So let us sound the music of our praises.*

Back at the car, Mandy opened the trunk while I settled Lili into her car seat. Mandy walked around to Tavi's side, opened the door, and held up two bobbing blue "Little Mister Warwick" balloons.

"Balloons!" shouted Tavi.

"A souvenir," said Mandy.

"Where did you get those?" I asked.

"I spotted them in the hotel when I came down to start loading up the car. They were tied to a couple of chairs, and they didn't seem to belong to anyone, so I took them."

Lili looked worried. "But I don't want to hurt the ducks."

"The ducks?" asked Mandy.

"What Mommy said about the ducks. How they swallow the balloons and die."

"There's nothing to worry about. I'm going to be very careful with these balloons, and tie them down tightly, so they won't fly away." Mandy was busy tying each one to a backpack as she spoke. "There. The ducks are safe."

Mandy and I embraced before getting into the car.

"Thank you," I said. "You were right—it was a great weekend."

"It wasn't exactly the weekend I imagined," said Mandy.

"No. Nonetheless."

And we set off for home.

"Ahh," I let out a deep breath. "'Mid pleasures and palaces, though we may roam, be it ever so humble, there's no place like home.'"

MY FATHER'S WIFE
AND MY DAUGHTER'S EMU

1. The Wife

My father lay on his bed in the nursing home, propped up with some pillows behind him. He wore his favorite black polo shirt and a pair of tan corduroys, a couple of sizes too big for his diminished frame. He seemed to like the feel of the material: the fingers of his left hand were in motion rubbing a small area just under his hip. His beard— its color the same faded pale orange-white as his hair—had grown quite long. The nurse at the desk had warned me about that. Apparently he was waiting to get a shave from his barber back in New York.

It had been some time since I had first brought him to the nursing home. The staff had suggested I give him a couple of months to adjust to being there, because from the moment he arrived he had been extremely angry with me and vehement that I take him back to New York. When I visited him or we spoke on the phone, he had only one thing on his mind: I needed to drive him back to New York City. He didn't belong in this place, he had business to take care of in Manhattan, this was a place for old people, crazy people. He was not one of them. New York City. Yes, he missed New York, but what he really missed was himself. And I could not restore himself to him.

I was in touch with the social worker. She said it usually goes one of two ways: "They're angry at you or they're angry at us." She laughed. "It works better for us when they're angry at you." She agreed it made sense for me to wait on visiting him. In the meantime I worked on the practical matters—filing the Medicaid application, rerouting his social security checks from Adult Protective Services to the new nursing home, selecting a Medicare Part D plan, and unknotting various past financial tangles. Periodically I dropped in for a visit, testing the waters.

The room was spare, with a single framed photo of my daughters on his night table and a local bank calendar hanging on the wall behind a scruffy wooden chair. Stacks of newspapers and magazines spilled over onto the floor. His was the bed near the door; he had a roommate whose bed was curtained off, but the roommate himself was never there during the day. The staff brought everybody out of their rooms to sit in the common area. Everybody except my father, that is, who insisted on staying on his bed, in his room.

"Nomi!" He was surprised to see me.

"How're you doing, Dad?"

"Terrible. You must take me back to New York. I can't stay here. I have business to take care of." He was so angry he almost shook. I'd been hoping things would be different.

"Dad, I know you want to go back to New York—"

"You know?" He raised his voice. "Then do something.

I have urgent business matters to attend to." Little drops of saliva sprayed from his mouth, which he wiped with the back of his hand. "Besides, my wife is in New York—she doesn't know where I am. I'm sure she's worried about me."

The wife was new. I didn't know what to make of the wife. "Dad, are you sure you have a wife?"

"What are you talking about? Of course I have a wife." He searched for the words to describe his wife. "She's a very important person in New York. She runs a hospital and an apartment building. Three apartment buildings. One of them with a pool." Talking about the importance of his wife seemed to have a slight calming effect on him. Maybe it was the swimming pool.

"I'm not sure I've met her."

"What are you talking about? Are you stupid? Of course you've met her." Now he was scornful in addition to being angry.

What could I do but enter into the delusion? "Oh, yeah, maybe I have. What's her name again?"

We couldn't, either of us, come up with her name. Well, names are sometimes hard to remember. In my childhood, my father always mixed up the names of my sisters and myself. It was understandable that the name of his wife would escape him. After all, he had been divorced twice and had countless other involvements. Daughters, wives, lovers, prostitutes—the names of the women in one's life could be difficult to keep track of.

I suggested a few names, women he had mentioned over the years. "Charlotte? Giselle? Sharon?" None of them were right. "Debbie?" He paused, tasted the name in his mouth. "I think that's it," he finally said. "Yes, Debbie.

You're right." He pointed at me in approval with his bent, bony finger, the nail too long and dirty.

"Hey, Dad, your fingernails. Do they need cutting? That one looks kind of long." And filthy, I didn't add.

He examined his nails. "You're right—they're too long. Will you cut them?"

I wasn't sure. I hadn't wanted to be directly responsible for his personal care. Yet it was a simple, a necessary thing, and it gave us something to do—a way to relate that didn't have to do with discussions about my driving him back to New York.

"Do you have a nail clipper?"

He searched about him for a nail clipper, patting his pockets and the mattress where he lay. "I don't have one," he said.

"Could there be one in a drawer? Or in the bathroom? If you can't find one, I can bring one in the next time I come...."

He opened the small drawer of his night table. Inside were the slips of paper that he had used to request his meals each day since arriving at the nursing home: little forms with boxes checked off for the various items: cereal versus toast, for example. Orange juice or milk. Coffee or tea. Etcetera. "See these," he reached for one of the slips and showed it to me. "I keep all of these."

"Do you really need to keep those, Dad?"

"Yes, every one. In case there's a question on my bill."

I considered explaining to him that this was not a hotel—his meals were not billed according to what he ordered—but I didn't want to disturb whatever peace he had made with the food at this place, or just now with me.

"Any nail clippers in there?"

"Right. Nail clippers." He peered into the drawer, shuffling the slips of paper about. "Nope. No nail clippers. I can ask at the desk."

With great concentration he rolled to one side and slowly swung his legs over the edge of the bed, searched with his feet for his slippers, stood up, and shuffled to the door.

He returned with a nail clipper in hand and sat down on his bed. I proceeded to cut his fingernails. I took his frail hand in mine, the skin surprisingly soft. When I was young, he had taken meticulous care of his fingernails, scrubbing them each day with a nailbrush when he returned home from work in the evening. I liked to kneel on the toilet, leaning against the sink to watch. Sometimes he would scrub my nails, too, with the same brush, which poked and tickled, and made a thick froth of the soap. Now, one by one, I carefully clipped his yellowing fingernails. We both stared at the little crescent slivers that fell onto the newspaper that I had placed in his lap. For once he had forgotten his urgent need for me to return him to New York. And in the relief from his constant demand, I only at this moment fully comprehended the sad truth that I hadn't previously acknowledged to myself: my father would *never* go back to New York again. The city he loved. His adoptive home.

I didn't wait very long before returning to see him again.

"Hello, Dad." I walked over to where he half lay, half sat on his bed and we kissed on each cheek, the French way, and then an extra kiss on the first cheek, which had always been his way (he was French, but I've never known

179

whether the third kiss was a regional thing or just his). His cheeks were rough with several days' growth of white and carroty orange beard. He had finally let one of the nurses trim his beard.

"How are you doing?" I asked as I cleared the wooden chair of its newspapers so I could sit down.

"Terrible. I can't stand it here. I have to get back to New York. I need you to help me."

I braced myself for the customary onslaught, but he surprised me. "I don't need you to drive me."

"You don't?"

"My wife is coming to get me. But I need you to call her for me."

"You want me to call her?"

"Yes. And tell her she needs to call me, and to come no later than Wednesday."

"Do you have her phone number?"

"I do have it. I don't know where it is. You don't have it?"

I was delighted that the responsibility for driving him back to New York had shifted from me to his wife. I didn't want the plan to fall through just because we couldn't come up with his wife's phone number.

"I must have it at home," I said.

"Where is your home?"

"Right here in Northampton."

He looked blankly at me. Did he know that "here" was Northampton? After a pause, during which time he seemed to dismiss that inscrutable piece of information as unnecessary to his plan, he continued. "So you can call her from home. And then call me to let me know what she said."

I thought quickly. I did not want to start having to call him regularly with updates from his wife. "I'll call you only if I reach her."

"You will reach her."

"I don't know—she's a busy person. All those apartment buildings to manage. And the hospital. Not to mention the swimming pool. Quite a responsibility."

He pulled at his lips, giving that some thought.

"If you don't reach her, leave her a message. Remember, she has to come by Wednesday."

"Right. Wednesday."

"At the latest."

"I'll call you if I reach her. If I don't reach her, I'll try to leave a message for her. I'll only call you if I reach her."

Satisfied with himself and with my response, he had nothing more to say. And I didn't know what to say. Now that we had moved away from the predominant subject of our relationship—his desire for me to drive him back to New York—we would have to find new conversational territory. We were suddenly shy with each other.

"What else?" I said.

"What else," he echoed, his voice trailing off.

2. The Emu

When I returned home, my younger daughter, nine-year-old Lili, had finished her homework and was interested in hanging out with me.

"Great," I said. "What should we do?" In her hand she held her favorite stuffed animal, the small and very appealing baby emu that she had named Emmy.

"You decide," Lili said. We were sitting in the living room, on our purple L-shaped sofa, she on one end, and I

181

on the far end of the other side. She threw Emmy at me, and I threw Emmy back to her.

"We can do whatever you'd like," I said. "But you have to decide."

"I don't know. I can't decide."

"Should we list some possibilities?"

"You list them," she said, throwing Emmy to me once more.

I thought Emmy looked a bit like Lili, with her skinny legs, long neck, beaked nose, wide-set eyes, and dark feathery hair. I held Emmy up, legs dangling, and turned her to face toward Lili.

"Lili," I said, in a squeaky voice. "This is boring. Mommy shouldn't decide. You figure out what you want to do."

And that was the first time Emmy spoke. But it would not be the last.

Lili brightened. "Emmy, what do *you* want to do?"

"Me?" I answered for Emmy. "How would I know what to do? I'm only an emu. You're going to have to come up with an idea on your own." I threw Emmy back to Lili.

Lili spoke to Emmy. "You're just saying that because it's what Mommy thinks."

"Well, obviously," said Emmy. Lili pounded Emmy's head with her fist.

"Ouch. Stop that. That's what you want to do? Just sit here and beat up on me? That's your idea of a fun time?"

"Well..." Lili shrugged and pounded Emmy's head once more, a big grin on her face. We both started to laugh, both she and I, that is. Emmy wasn't amused.

"You two are mean," Emmy said. "And you're ganging up on me."

"Oh Emmy, I love you." Lili kissed Emmy on the top of her feathery head.

"Well you have a funny way of showing it."

The phone rang. I got up and checked to see who was calling. It was the nursing home. Was something wrong?

"Hello," I answered in a high-pitched voice, realizing too late that I had just answered the phone as Emmy.

It was Jody, the very kind nurse on my father's unit. My father wanted to talk to me. Would I speak with him? She put him on.

"Nomi?"

"Hello, Daddy. What's up?"

"I was just checking to see if you called my wife."

I wasn't quite sure how to respond. "I called her but I didn't reach her," I said.

"Are you sure you had the right number?"

"Yes, I'm pretty sure."

"What was the number?"

"What was the number?" I had thought it was clever to say I knew the number. I hadn't imagined he would make me prove it to him. "I don't remember—I would have to look it up again. 212 something..."

"Okay, I'll wait. You look it up."

Although I could have just made up some random phone number, for some reason I thought I should strive for a certain degree of verisimilitude. So I carried the phone with me to my study and fished in my filing cabinet for the folder from The House (his old residence, a single-room-occupancy hotel in Manhattan).

"OK, Dad, here it is." Finding the main switchboard number, one I used to call to reach him, or, more often, to reach the social worker, I read it off to him.

"Yes! That's right! That's the number. So, did you leave a message?" he asked.

"Well..." Here I wasn't sure. Should I say I left a message? Would he then expect to receive a phone call from his wife at the nursing home? For how long would his diminished mind remember all of this? Or should I just say there was no machine, and I'd keep trying to reach her? And I'd let him know when I did? It could be a very long time. An important woman like that, she might be extremely hard to reach. "Nobody picked up, and there was no answering machine, so I couldn't leave a message."

"What are you talking about? Of course there's a machine."

"Well, it wasn't working, maybe. The phone just kept ringing. I'll keep trying."

"It's very strange."

"I'll let you know when I reach her. You don't need to call me again." That was the key piece of information I wanted him to retain. "You can wait for me to call you. I love you, Dad."

"Love you, too. Good-bye."

I hadn't noticed that Lili and Emmy had followed me up to my study. When I spun my chair around, Lili stood holding Emmy straight out in front of her, about one foot from my face. Neither of them said anything. I understood from Lili's insistent posture, not moving, not speaking, that Lili wished for Emmy to say something.

"You want Emmy to speak?" I suddenly felt extremely fatigued, trapped simultaneously by my father's wife and my daughter's emu.

Without saying anything, Lili retracted the hand that held Emmy and then pushed it forward again.

"Lili just because Emmy's not saying anything, it doesn't mean you can't."

Lili remained silent.

"Cat got your tongue?" asked Emmy.

"Hunh?"

"Did the cat get your tongue?" repeated Emmy.

"What does that mean? What cat?" asked Lili.

I snatched Emmy from Lili's hand so she could point to Lili's mouth with her beak. "It's an expression for when someone's not talking. Like you weren't," said Emmy.

"How does Emmy know that expression?"

"I know everything Mommy knows. Mommy and I, we have a special kind of telepathic thing going. So, are we going to play a game or what?"

Thus on the same day I became saddled with both my daughter's and my father's expectations that I would somehow meet the narrative demands that arose from their yearnings.

3. The Wife and the Emu

First thing upon arriving home from school every day, Lili would remove Emmy from her little lawn chair (it had belonged to a Barbie doll) that sat on the front hall table (where Emmy presumably lay dreaming about Lili all day, awaiting her return), and would then hold Emmy up in front of my face. I could see that what I had thought a clever little idea, acted on spontaneously in a light moment—to speak as Emmy—was taking hold inside Lili with unanticipated consequences. What could I do but continue to be Emmy's voice? Of course, many children animate their stuffed animals. Some do it by talking for them. Others imagine they hear them talking. Probably a handful actually do hear them talking. But my daughter's way was to wait for me to make Emmy speak. At bedtime, especially, speaking with Emmy became an expected and essential part of Lili's routine.

While Lili brushed her teeth, Emmy and I closed the curtains in her room. We climbed up into the top bunk of Lili's bunk bed to wait for her. The three of us would hang out together, snuggling in bed and shooting the breeze, until Emmy reminded Lili that it was time to go to sleep.

"No, don't leave."

Emmy reasoned with her. "Lili, it's a school night. You'll be tired if Mommy doesn't leave right now."

"I don't care."

"You may not care, but in the morning when Mommy has to cajole you out of bed and then drive you to the bus stop if you take too long, she's not going to be very friendly. You know how Mommy gets."

"Hey, Emmy, be nice," I said.

"Yeah, Emmy. Be nice to Mommy," Lili chimed in.

"Well, just saying," Emmy said. "Mommy and I will both be nice if you go to sleep right now."

I appreciated Emmy's refreshing lack of inhibition and self-censorship, as she had no qualms about speaking her mind. I enjoyed disagreeing with her and took great pleasure no matter the outcome: when either one of us won the argument, or when together we came to some mutual understanding. I never worried about hurting Emmy's feelings, because I knew she was tough-skinned and could handle it. I found that whereas speaking as Emmy often felt like a burden, requiring a level of energy I couldn't always muster, it also sometimes became a welcome creative outlet.

As for my father, Wednesday passed and I was never able to contact his wife. I felt reluctant to visit him again because I didn't know how much he had been counting on the wife to come get him, and therefore how upset he would be that I hadn't reached her. I let a couple of weeks go by, and then I found that putting off seeing him didn't feel very good either. I called the nursing home and asked Jody, the nurse on duty, if it would be a good day for a visit. In her always kind and friendly way she encouraged me to stop by. She said my father seemed in good spirits. I biked over that morning.

"He's in his room," Jody said with a nod toward his door. "He knows you're coming."

It turned out that it didn't seem to have registered that the Wednesday deadline for the wife had long since passed. He was thick in his plan, which had become more elaborate, involving somebody else coming up a few days before his wife, to pack up his things. He was still expecting me to call her.

Our visits took on a regular pattern. Always the plan, the wife, New York. His wife. I was interested in her. I wondered whether my father had an actual person in mind, or if she was purely a figment of his imagination. If I attributed certain characteristics to the wife or referred to an accomplishment of hers of my own invention, would my father go along with it, or would he tell me it wasn't so? How real was she to him? How fleshed out was his fantasy? I tried to ask him about her, but he was fixated exclusively on her role in his plan. Once again I started to avoid visiting my father because even though he was no longer angry, he was persistent in his demands. It was exhausting to keep putting him off, trying to change the subject or redirect him. I felt like shouting, Stop with the wife. There is no wife. The nursing staff said he was doing fine, but I was not doing fine. I decided to take another break.

A new development arose with Lili and Emmy: Lili pulled out a couple of Playmobil props and set them up near Emmy's lawn chair on the front hall table where Emmy always sat when Lili was away from home.

When Lili first received her as a present for her seventh birthday, Emmy immediately became Lili's favorite stuffed animal, and Lili took her everywhere, even to school (although at school she had to keep Emmy in her cubby or backpack, taking her out only at break time). Some of Lili's friends regularly brought their stuffed animals into school as well, and Emmy quickly developed a friendship circle of her own, being especially fond of a muskrat named Junior Muskrat. As Lili grew older she stopped taking Emmy to school, and after a scare when Emmy fell off the bleachers at a particularly exciting moment of a softball game where Lili and I had been watching her older sister Tavi play—and then we all went home without realizing that Emmy was not in my jacket pocket where Lili had put her for safe-keeping—Lili rarely took Emmy anywhere. (I rushed back to the softball field as soon as we noticed she was missing and found her lying on the ground beneath the bleacher seats, undamaged by her fall, but—as we were later to find out when Emmy began to speak—pissed off that we had left her there. Emmy had a lot to say about the incident and invoked it at those moments where she felt wronged or neglected.) I was glad that as a result of that experience Lili almost always left her at home. Emmy had seemingly become what one might call agoraphobic. And because Emmy never went outside, it meant the conversations with Emmy took place only in the privacy of our home. I never had to worry about speaking the voice of Emmy in a public place with other people around to hear her/me.

The Playmobil props seemed innocuous enough. When I noticed the set-up I commented on it to Lili.

"How nice that Emmy has something to do now when she's sitting in her chair," I said, admiring the little computer, the violin, the telephone, the book, the glass complete with a straw, the piece of cake set out nicely on a plate, and the beautiful vase of purple flowers.

"Do you know what this means?" Lili asked, pointing to the phone.

"It means that Emmy can call 911 in case of an emergency?"

"No, Mommy. That's ridiculous." Lili gave me a little shove. "It means that when I'm not here I can call Emmy and talk to her on the telephone." I should have realized what Lili was planning, but in the moment, I didn't fully digest what she had just said.

The next day, as I was walking Lili home from school, Lili said, "I'm going to call Emmy on the phone." She lifted her hand as though it had a phone in it, and pantomimed pushing the buttons. "E-M-M-Y I'm calling Emmy. E-M-M-Y. Hello Emmy, are you there?" She looked at me with that expectant look she always had on her face when she held Emmy up in front of me waiting for me to say something.

We lived near a big park, and we were walking along

its grassy edge, with groups of children and their parents scattered about not far from us. "Here? You want Emmy to speak right here? You can't wait until we get home?"

"Hello Emmy, are you there?" Lili repeated.

"I think the line is busy," I said. "I think Emmy's already on the phone with somebody else."

"Who would Emmy be talking to?" Lili asked.

I thought about it. "Maybe Emmy's talking to my father's wife Debbie."

Lili glared at me. "Your father doesn't have a wife."

"Okay. Then she's talking to my father."

"Your father doesn't have a phone."

"True. But he has access to the phone at the nurses' station." Though I had started it, this conversation was clearly absurd and also now making me uncomfortable, because I had been avoiding my father and his wife. I stopped walking and cocked my head slightly. "All right, I think Emmy's off the phone now."

"E-M-M-Y. I'm calling Emmy. Emmy are you there?"

"Hello," I squeaked, looking around to see if anyone was close enough to hear me.

From then on, when I was out with Lili, Lili took to calling Emmy on the telephone. Just as my father only wanted to talk to me about calling his wife, when I was with Lili, she only wanted me to speak as Emmy. And now she found a way for that to happen even when Emmy wasn't actually there. It was getting to be too much for me.

A period of self-doubt ensued. Was it wrong for me to continue in this way? Was there something wrong with Lili's reliance on me to speak as Emmy? Again and again I suggested that Lili try speaking for Emmy herself, but Lili steadfastly refused. If my own creativity flourished through Emmy, was it getting in the way of Lili's? Was I spoiling her by capitulating to her desire for entertainment? Had Lili found a clever substitute for the mind-numbing television shows we had made certain she never watched? No cable? No problem! I'll turn on Mommy. Me! As Emmy! Or was it just that Lili wanted a way to connect with me? Was that so wrong? Speaking as Emmy I was engaging and irreverent. Fun! Why shouldn't she want Emmy there constantly? It's possible that Lili had figured out that Emmy brought out my best, most light-hearted self.

My father began to call me daily on the phone, and when I didn't pick up, he left messages: "Nomi, this is your father. You must call my wife. You must tell her to call me. And call me right back."

I needed to stop his phone calls, and I needed to do something about his constant expectation that I would call his wife. I could see no other solution: it seemed my father's wife would have to die. And it would be up to me to make it happen.

On my way over to the Care Center I rehearsed what I would say. Dad, terrible news. The reason why your wife has been so hard to reach on the phone, with no way to leave a message? It's that, I'm so sorry, but she's passed away.

My father was lying on his bed and we made our usual greeting. I cleared off the wooden chair and sat down, taking a deep breath.

"So, Nomi, it's all coming together. My wife has

become one of the directors here at this, this..." He couldn't find the word for what this was.

"This place?" I offered.

"Well, you could call it that..." He had been searching for a different word. "Anyway, that means she has some money coming to her, a lot of money." I couldn't quite follow what he was saying, preoccupied as I was with the sad news I was about to share with him.

"Dad?"

"What?"

"I have some terrible news."

"What is it?"

"Your wife, Debbie, I learned that she's very sick." I couldn't quite do it. At the last minute I couldn't manage to have her just up and die without any warning.

My father's reaction was completely unexpected. He put one hand up to his cheek and shook his head.

"I know, I know," he said. "She's always had this problem, with the drugs. She's an addict. Is it very bad? And the pneumonia? Has it gotten worse?"

I had no idea what to say. His eyes welled up with tears.

"Dad I'm sorry, I'm so sorry."

I sat down beside him and took one of his hands in mine, and we sat there together, saying nothing. I had no idea whether this Debbie was an actual person in his life, or who had once been in his life, whether she was someone he had befriended or even been involved with when he lived at The House, or whether she was simply made up. That his wife, who owned a hospital and three apartment buildings—one with a swimming pool—turned out to have a drug problem, was shocking to me.

That night when Lili and Emmy and I were hanging out before bedtime, Lili asked me if I could imitate Emmy.

"What?" I wasn't sure I had understood her correctly.

"Can you imitate Emmy?" she repeated.

I considered my response. "I think I do what you might call a perfect imitation of Emmy."

Lili grinned. "*I* can imitate Emmy," she said.

I tried to take in the meaning of this. I wasn't exactly sure what to make of it, but it seemed to me that Lili's interest in speaking as Emmy, even if it was only in imitation of me, might be a first step toward finding her own voice.

"Can you really imitate me?" Emmy squeaked.

"Can you really imitate me?" Lili squeaked.

"You sound just like me," said Emmy.

"You sound just like me," Lili repeated.

It was true: Lili did a great Emmy imitation.

"Wow," I said. "You do a fantastic imitation of Emmy. So fantastic, it could be Emmy herself speaking. I would never know the difference."

We let that sink in. I wasn't quite sure what to make of it. I had been worried that Lili never wanted to speak for Emmy. And now finally she had tried her hand at it, except that she wasn't actually using her own voice but imitating mine instead. Is that how we all begin to find our own voice? By finding someone else's voice first?

Then Lili had another question for me. "Can Emmy imitate you?" she asked.

I tried, but I found it impossible to do my own regular voice as it might sound if it were coming from Emmy's higher-pitched voice.

"Impossible," I said. "I give up. Can you imitate me?"

"Why would I want to?" Lili replied.

I returned to visit my father the very next day, worried about how he was doing. He was unusually cheerful. He made no mention of our conversation the previous day, or his tears. Good news! His wife was going to come up and visit for a week. He didn't say a word about her taking him back to New York, or about me calling her. He said nothing about the pneumonia or her addiction to drugs. It was as though we had not had that conversation the day before.

What was I thinking? Of course it was as though the conversation had never happened. Given my father's diminishing memory, it might as well not have happened. Certainly as far as my father was concerned, it hadn't happened. If I thought I could have any control at all over the narrative of his wife, or his life, I was deluded. His wife was a product of his mind. His mind invented her, and his mind, not mine, would determine what happened to her.

"I hope that you'll be able to stop by to see her when she's here," my father said. "I know she would like that very much."

"As would I," I said. "I look forward to it." Who knows? Maybe his wife would manage to find her way up here from New York. And if she did, might it be interesting to introduce my father's wife to my daughter's emu? There was really no way to predict whether they would get along.

MY FATHER'S STORY

Our kitchen was a small room shaped like a keyhole. My father sat at the table, fiercely smoking a cigarette between sloppy gulps of coffee.

"Where's Mom?" I asked.

"Your mother isn't home."

"Maybe I'll wait for her to come back before I make my breakfast. Was she going to get bagels?" There was a bakery nearby called Mother's that also made a very nice caraway rye and a great pumpernickel raisin bread.

My father wiped his mouth with a paper napkin. A little piece of the napkin tore off and clung to the faint carrot-colored stubble on his chin—it wasn't like him not to shave first thing in the morning, even on a Sunday. "She's not going to come back just yet. Your mother didn't come home last night."

"What?" I sat down a few chairs away from him. The table was round with a white laminated top. With my finger, I worked on erasing a coffee stain. "She didn't come home? Why not? Where is she?"

My father cupped his right hand under the ashes that were about to fall from his cigarette. "I wanted to talk to you before Leah wakes up. She's too young to hear this." He looked about for a place to put out his cigarette and finding none, took a last gulp of coffee and dropped both the cigarette and the ashes into his cup. The cigarette made a nice little hiss; a spiral of smoke rose above the lid of the cup. He lifted the cup by the handle and sloshed the cigarette around.

"I don't know what your mother's going to tell you when she gets home. I wanted to make sure you heard my side of this. I just spent a very unpleasant couple of hours listening to your mother make accusations against me. She said she found my body repulsive."

When my father gets excited and starts to talk faster, sometimes little bits of spit start spraying from his mouth. This was happening now. "She says I don't satisfy her. I'm telling you, we used to have a very satisfying sex life."

I was sixteen. I didn't want to hear about my parents' sex life.

"Lots of women find me attractive. And I've had plenty of opportunity, traveling on business, staying in hotels. But I never cheated on your mother. Your mother? She had an affair with Bernie Landers when you were ten years old. Did you know that? It's true. And he's not the only one. I just wanted to tell you what's what. I don't know what your mother's going to say when she gets home, but there are two sides to this thing."

My father pushed his chair back, making a scraping sound on the floor, and nearly tipping it over backwards. He picked up his coffee cup and brought it over to the sink. He turned the faucet on full force, turned it off, and grabbed the kitchen towel to dry his shirt and pants where the water had splashed. When he tried to return the towel to its hook, it fell to the floor.

That was how it began. For two years, my parents stayed together. Sometimes my mother went away for a weekend. She would give me a telephone number, in case I needed to reach her. I wasn't allowed to give the number to my father.

He started to lose his temper. A Sunday evening, my mother just back from a weekend away. We're in the kitchen, getting dinner ready. My father sits slicing the steak with a large knife, a glass of scotch close at hand. My mother fixes a salad—she's drinking Jack Daniels. Leah sets the table while I get the drinks. Beer for my parents, soda for us. I flick the radio off on my way to the table. He says, "I'm listening to the radio." I hate listening to the radio while we eat. My father knows that. He turns it back on. We repeat this. "Can't we keep the radio off during dinner?" I plead. "I want it on," and he turns up the volume, then lifts the radio up to a higher shelf so I can't reach it. "FUCK," I scream. I was very careful not to say, "Fuck *you*." The distinction is lost on him. "Don't you curse at me." He stands up, carving knife still in his hand, and walks toward me. I back away into the hallway. He approaches me, pushing aside a chair in his path, the knife still in his hand. The knife: I thought he was going to cut me with the knife. Instead, he hits me across the face with his other hand. "Don't you ever talk to me like that," he shouts. I can see my mother watching through the doorway. "Aren't you going to say something? Are you going to just let him do that?" I scream at her. She has a curious expression on her face—is it satisfaction? Vindication?

When he was not in a fury, he spent hours lying on top of his bed in the dark with his clothes on, including his shoes. He told me he was thinking about killing himself.

Divorce made my mother frightening in a way that was completely consistent with the person I already knew her to be. She had always wanted things and had always gone after them. She set up a Buddhist shrine in her bedroom and chanted "*nom yo ho ren gey kyo*," hoping it would bring men into her life. When it did, she dismantled the shrine and stopped chanting. My father became other than who he was. There was chaos floating around the edges of my family, but my parents' marriage had provided a container that kept it at bay. Then my mother decided she wanted to end the marriage. And my father lost his tether.

She vowed to change the locks if he didn't leave our apartment. I was home from my first year of college. She had set a date—June 1—and if he hadn't moved out by then he would come home from work and find out that his key didn't fit in the lock anymore. She wasn't going to tell him about it; she was just going to do it. As the date approached, my sisters and I circled ads in the classified section and left the paper in his room. We offered to go look at places with him. I have some leads, he would say. I've been asking around. He couldn't afford his own apartment, but he heard about a room for rent in somebody's house—a widow, an older woman whose husband had played bridge with one of his bridge partners. Sounds good, we said. We can help you pack. It's just a room, he said, there's not a lot to pack. One night, toward the end of May, my mother went into his bedroom—she had long before moved into my room—and closed the door. We could hear raised voices. On the following Saturday, my father packed up his clothes, some manila file folders, and his toiletries. We trailed behind him while he carried a couple of suitcases and boxes down to the car. It was an unusually hot and sticky day; the heat pressed in on us as we stepped out from the cool lobby of our building. He carefully wiped the sweat from his face with his folded handkerchief and kissed us good-bye. Then he shook open the handkerchief as though he were about to perform a magic trick, slowly refolded it, put it back in his pocket, and rolled down the windows before climbing into his car and driving away.

"I'll get him for this," my mother hung up the phone, hard. "That bastard."

"Who was it? What did they say?"

"The police found my car. They said it wasn't stolen."

My mother had left our apartment to go to work and five minutes later came back up to tell me that our car had been stolen. It wasn't in the place she had parked it the night before. Now the police were saying it wasn't stolen.

"It wasn't stolen? Then what happened to it?"

"It was impounded. Your father hasn't made a payment in six months. The bank impounded it." She reached for her purse. "Come on."

In a car borrowed from a friend, we drove over to my father's place. To my relief, his car wasn't in the driveway. My mother was in a rant. I had no idea what she was planning to do.

"You know what he does? I'll tell you what he does. He gets a bill in the mail, he doesn't want to deal with it, he just doesn't open it. As though it doesn't exist if he doesn't look at it. That's how he lives his life." As she got out of the car, she continued, "I'm going to find those bills. Who knows what else he hasn't paid for?"

She started walking up the driveway. "How will you get in?" I called from the car.

"Mrs. Eliasoph will let me in." The widow whose spare room my father was renting. "She knows me." She stopped walking, turned around and got back into the car. "Maybe I shouldn't bother her. I bet he's at that woman's house." My mother had learned from a friend that my father was seeing a woman. She put the car into reverse. "That's where he is. I'll go find him there. She should learn what kind of person he is."

"Let's not look for him there. I'm sure he's not there. I bet he's at work."

"You're right. The bus stop. I bet he parked near the express bus." She was like a wind-up toy, pointing first in one direction, then another.

As we approached, we could see the old white Chevy station wagon parked along the street. My mother pulled up behind it, opened her door before the car had come to a full stop. "I'll get him," she shouted. "I'll get him." She ran from door to door, opening them all, popped up the hood, lifted the rear hatch. She was going to exact her revenge on him through this car. "I'll get that bastard." As though the car were a totem. She pulled open the glove compartment, dumped the contents, twisted the rear-view mirror, released the hood. She poked around under the hood and removed something, some kind of round rusty metal pan, like a flat jello mold, and stood there holding it. "This is stupid," she said. "I have no idea what this is." She closed up the car and we drove back home.

My mother had chanted to find another man, but my father had no problem finding other women. By the time I was twenty-eight he had been through several relationships, had remarried and was again divorced, living on his own in a two-bedroom apartment in Queens that he had shared with his second wife and her daughter. I myself had fallen in love with a woman named Mandy and was living with her in Northampton.

My father's second marriage: what natural process would best describe it? It was an avalanche waiting to happen. Chilly. Dangerous conditions. Ill-advised. Or no, a brewing category five hurricane, picking up more warm, wet air as it headed toward land. By the time it was over, his wife would be chasing him with a knife in the airport, and they would each have taken a restraining order out against the other.

During most of his second marriage I had seen little of him, but now I arranged for a visit. I was going to be in the city visiting friends. I planned to spend the night at my father's and have breakfast with him before heading back home, to Northampton. I arrived at about ten o'clock and tried the doorbell. When there was no answer, I let myself in with the key he had left under the doormat.

"Dad?" I called out, tentatively. I reached for the light switch. "Daddy?"

I wandered down the narrow hallway. A dim light beckoned me into a room off to the right. My father was asleep in an armchair; his head leaned heavily on his chest, distorting his face. His breath was heavy and rhythmic. Two fingers of his left hand held a worm of cigarette ash. An empty bottle of Dewars stood on the floor beside the lit lamp.

"Dad?" I said once more. "I'm here." He was clearly in a deep, drunken sleep, and I hesitated before leaning over him to shake his arm. When he roused himself and looked up at me, there was a look in his eyes I had never seen before: a look I felt I shouldn't be seeing. "You're a beautiful woman," he said, slurring the words. The ash between his fingers fell to the ground as he reached both hands up to grab my head and bring it toward his face. His mouth looked red and wet. "Kiss me," he said. I pulled away.

With a great effort he lifted himself and stood; swaying, he tried to steady himself by reaching one hand out toward the frayed upholstery of the chair back. "You're a beautiful woman," he repeated. That look. "Why won't you kiss me?"

I fled and spent the night in the second bedroom, with the door locked and barricaded, lying awake in the dark, listening for the sound of his footsteps. The next morning, he sat at the kitchen table, studying a pile of old black and white photographs. "Good morning," he said, looking up at me.

"I'm going," I said.

"Going already? Don't you want some breakfast?" His voice was normal, and he didn't appear to be drunk at all. He picked up one of the pictures and stared at it. "Your grandmother," he said. "She was such a beautiful woman. What a beautiful woman," and held his hand out to show me the picture. I couldn't bear to look at it.

When I was a child, everyone in my family told me I looked just like my father's mother. I thought I looked nothing like her. It had something to do with her skin, which was very light. My father was red-headed and his skin was also light. My mother's skin was dark. But it was more than my grandmother's skin. There was something about me that reminded them of her.

My grandmother died of colon cancer when I was four. I didn't understand my mother's explanations of colon cancer, but what sense I made of it was that something had been blocking up the inside of my grandmother, so she wasn't able to poop. Sometimes I had trouble pooping, and I believed this meant that, being so much like my grandmother, I was surely going to die of colon cancer the way she had.

We were vacationing on Cape Cod, sitting around the small kitchen table staring at my father as he shouted into the phone, "*Das ist ein area code. Ya. Nein.*" I was fourteen. He wore only his bathing suit, baggy blue and tan checkered boxer shorts. It looked like he was wearing a t-shirt: the skin where his t-shirt had covered it was very pale in contrast to the reddened skin of his neck and arms. After a while, he let the phone fall into its cradle and turned to us. "Well," he said. "My father's dead." I looked at his eyes to see if any tears would come. They did not. I glanced at my mother to see how I should react, but she seemed uncertain, too. She did not reach out to my father. He fumbled with a pack of cigarettes: picked them up, tried to reach inside the small opening to fish one out. His fingers were too broad and too clumsy. He hit the edge of the pack against the edge of the table with two sharp thwacks, and when a cigarette poked out, he lifted the whole pack up to his mouth to grab it with his lips. His matchbook was empty. We watched him at the stove as he bent over to light his cigarette from the burner. Then he walked out of the room, leaving behind him the sharp echo of the tightly sprung screen door slamming shut.

My partner Mandy and I named our first daughter after my father's mother. Three-month-old Tavi slept peacefully in her car seat on the chair next to mine. We were in a restaurant I had never been to—upscale, quiches and salads. Mood lighting. My only task now in life was to protect Tavi. Such a relief, for life finally to be so well-defined. We sat—Mandy, our daughter Tavi, and I—on one side of the table, with my father and Charlotte across from us. Charlotte was the latest woman in his life. She had called inviting us to come out to the Berkshires, where she owned a house.

"There's plenty of room," she said. "You could stay over." I had never met Charlotte, and I hadn't seen my father in five years.

"Babies," said Mandy. "Everybody wants a piece of Tavi."

"And they can't have her! They can't have her!" I suddenly raised my voice.

Charlotte and my father made the trip to Northampton to see the baby. I became increasingly quiet at the restaurant, as my father downed one drink after another. Charlotte tried to carry the conversation. She alternately chewed and spoke and paused to swallow a sip of water with a practiced, confident ease. Driven by the clarity of purpose that Tavi provided, I felt a pure anger at my father rise inside me as I looked down at my quiche, dissecting it with my fork. Finally, even Charlotte stopped talking. Tavi stirred. I had to deposit the anger in my quiche before I looked at her so that I would look at her with only love in my eyes. I stabbed the quiche with my fork and left the fork standing upright, then turned to Tavi. Her eyes fluttered. I unclasped the buckle and lifted her toward me. For three months I had been nursing Tavi unselfconsciously wherever we happened to be. Not here. Not in front of my father. Tavi rooted against my collarbone. I stood up. Looked around. "I'm taking her to the bathroom," I said quietly to Mandy.

The bathroom smelled of a falsely fragrant chemical air sanitizer. "Sorry, Tavi," I said. "It stinks in here. It is disgusting to have to eat in the bathroom. I apologize." I sat on the toilet, propped her against my arm, eased my breast into her mouth. "Sorry, Tavi, sorry, sorry, sorry. I cannot let my father see my breast. I'm sorry."

Back at the table, my father reached out with one finger toward her hand, and I pulled away. "I am not a child molester," he said. Then he raised his voice and repeated what he said. People sitting near us suddenly became quiet. "Don't accuse me of things," he shouted. "I never touched you." Mandy grabbed the car seat and the three of us left the restaurant.

My father left Charlotte because he felt she was too controlling. It was Charlotte who had convinced my father to see a psychiatrist. He was given a dual diagnosis of bipolar illness and alcoholism and prescribed Depakote.

He tried it for a while and then decided he didn't need medication. When she admonished him to stay on the Depakote, he left her.

Now he needed money. He hired a detective to help him track down information about certain relatives of his who had been killed in Poland during the war. He believed they had put money into some Swiss bank accounts, and that he was in line to inherit that money. He had hatched a scheme to take part in the class action suit against Swiss banks that Senator D'Amato of New York was orchestrating. The detective was unable to find the information my father needed for his Swiss bank account claim, but he did manage to find my father's stepmother, my grandfather's second wife Irena. She was not actually lost: she had been living all along in a two-bedroom apartment in a rent-stabilized building near Lincoln Center, not far from where my father himself was living. When my grandfather died, he left all his money to Irena, and after a failed attempt to contest the will, my father had not stayed in touch with her.

I remembered my step-grandmother as a sweet, plump woman with bleached blond hair, who wore tight-fitting European clothing and spoke with a strong accent. When the detective found her, she was ninety-two and beginning to suffer from dementia. My father found some dependable Polish-speaking home health aides to care for her. He also managed to have her sign over to him the legal power of attorney. By the time Irena died, my father had already moved into her rent-stabilized apartment and had spent a considerable amount of her money, including a down payment on an apartment in Paris. Within six months he would lose the Paris apartment, be evicted from the N.Y. apartment, and find a way to spend or lose the rest of her money, over half a million dollars.

One October afternoon some months after the eviction, the phone rang. It was a man named Arnold Mandelbaum, who said he used to be a neighbor of my father's, years ago. Hello, you don't know me, I want to talk to you about a personal matter: it's about your father.

He's dead, he's sick, it's happening, I thought. Somewhere in me I had been expecting such a phone call. Only—no. He's neither dead nor sick but he's in bad shape, what did Arnold call it? In dire straits. He informed me that my father was living on the Grand Concourse in the Bronx with a woman named Jacquelyn. It was down to these two, Arnold and Jacquelyn, taking care of my father. Arnold and Jacquelyn did not know each other but were linked through the shared burden of my father. They wanted desperately for the burden to shift to me, the daughter. Arnold was ninety-three years old and had given my father money. Jacquelyn wanted him out of her apartment. The phone calls continued—every week, then every day.

It is snowing snowing snowing. A winter storm. The phone rings. Another phone call from Jacquelyn. I don't want to talk to Jacquelyn again. She has a problem she wants me to fix. I can't fix her problem, which is that my father moved into her one-bedroom apartment at the end of the summer, promising it would be for no more than two weeks, and now it is winter and he won't leave. He smells. He runs up her phone bill and eats her food, and he smells. Smell, smell seeping all over the apartment, relentless smell. I can smell it from here, that stale putrid sick-making smell of someone who hasn't washed or changed his clothes in months. Every time she mentions it I want to scream, stop, I can take the rest of it, but please, not the part about the smell again. Maybe it's not the worst for her, but I think it is the worst for me; a hundred and fifty miles away I can't seem to get the smell out of my nose.

Last night I dreamed he had gotten a dictionary as an incentive for buying a bookshelf, and he was giving the dictionary to me. He's thinking of me.

He did have a dictionary I once wanted. It was a Webster's second edition, unabridged, very large. He won it in a spelling bee when he was young. He was on a team, and his friends made him take it home because they didn't want to carry it. I can't imagine he actually had much to do with winning the contest—English is not his native language—but I can imagine him as the one having to carry this too-heavy dictionary home. That is the father who would later eat the little pieces of soap offered up to him at Halloween, when Rachel and her friends had the idea to pretend the soap was candy, and all the other parents knew better than to fall for the trick. I can still picture him spitting the soap out in a little paper napkin, with a bewildered look on his face. The father who, left-handed, was forced as a child to use his right hand instead. The father I was walking with when we ran into one of my teachers on the street—suddenly nervous, self-conscious, obsequious, uncomfortable, out of place. He told a bad joke.

It is the father who, after finally getting his hands on

over half a million dollars from his dying stepmother, managed in less than half a year to lose it all, as well as her rent-controlled apartment. The father my mother met at fourteen, who stood up politely every time my grandmother entered the room despite the taunts from my mother's friends. The father whose father disinherited him. It is the father I feel sorry for. The father I have to cringe for. The father who smells.

That is not the father taking up residence in Jacquelyn's apartment, promising to leave with no intention to leave, the father who borrows money from ninety-three-year-old Arnold Mandelbaum knowing he'll never pay it back, who is mean, manipulative, takes advantage of kind people, and refuses to take responsibility for any of his actions. The one who drinks too much. The one who screams at me over the phone and hangs up on me. The father who hurt me. Who in a drunken stupor wanted to kiss me because—who knows? I reminded him of his mother?

He got the idea I would be sending him money. The check is in the mail, he told Jacquelyn, not only Jacquelyn but also Shoshana the Polish Jew in Paris whom he expected to join there, as well as Arnold Mandelbaum, the ninety-three-year-old who called to get the scoop on why he, Arnold, had to take care of my father instead of us, my father's daughters. Did my father actually believe I was sending him a check, or was it a line he had used so often in his life that he just kept using it? Jacquelyn wants me to come and get him from her apartment. She doesn't want to have to put him out on the street.

Adult Protective Services will take someone away if he

meets their two criteria: 1. He is mentally and/or physically impaired and because of these impairments is unable to manage his own resources, carry out the activities of daily living, or protect himself from abuse, neglect, exploitation or other hazardous situations without assistance from others, and 2. He has no one available, willing, and able to assist him responsibly.

The catch in this situation is the second one: he must not have any family to take care of him, or, he must refuse the help of the family. A complicated point. He would accept our help if it came in the form of money. But if it comes in the form of finding treatment, psychiatric services, case management, services for substance abuse, a representative payee, no, he will not only refuse, he will hang up in anger. We have tried that route many times, more times than I can explain to Jacquelyn or Arnold. And we have learned that money is not the answer.

I have coached Jacquelyn on how to sell this one to Adult Protective Services, based on the advice of a very friendly social worker with the Jewish Services for the Aged, Inna Stanislovsky. The thing I liked best about Inna Stanislovsky, apart from her soft Russian accent, was the way she seemed completely unsurprised by anything I told her: about my father, about me, the whole story.

The whole story.

Nobody will tell me the whole story. It begins well before I am born when my father's father moved his family to France from a small town called Pabienice, near Lodz, in Poland. My father was born in Paris, in 1929. My father's immediate family—his parents and older sister—were living in France when the war broke out, and managed to escape the round-up of foreign Jews when the Nazis occupied Paris. They found a way to leave occupied France, moving south to Nice, where they lived for a year before making their way to the United States, via Spain and Cuba. My father was thirteen when they arrived in the U.S. Most of the rest of his family did not survive the war in Poland.

Sometimes my father's sister would call and talk and talk, and I had learned from my parents to prop the phone up against a pillow or hang it on the back of a kitchen chair and let her keep talking. Any one of us could pick up the phone and listen to her going on—until eventually the talking would stop and we would hang up the phone. Her voice was hoarse and accented and would sometimes reach a high sustained pitch, impossible to understand, blurring French and English and Yiddish and Polish—but we never hung up the phone until she had stopped talking.

He sits in Jacquelyn's one-room apartment on the Grand Concourse, very depressed, unable to sleep, not eating much, not washing. Smelling. He is afraid of New York. He thinks there will be bombs. He is remembering the escape from Nazi-occupied Paris with his family when he was a child. He thinks New Yorkers are naïve and he thinks Bush is dangerous; when the war on Iraq starts, New York will be bombed. He feels desperate to get out, and Shoshana awaits him in Paris, which feels like safety to him. He has a French birth certificate, he was born there, so when he goes back, he will be eligible for National Health. The French will take care of him. Motherland. He calls me and demands money. He works himself into a rage and threatens to sever our relationship if I don't send him money. He works himself into such a rage, especially when I suggest he has a problem and may need some help, that he hangs up on me.

He is enraged: all he needed was the money for a ticket to Paris, and his problems would be solved. Shoshana was waiting for him to move in with her. He only needed to get there. A tempting thought—a one-way ticket to Paris. My sisters and I decided that though we were resolved not to give him money, since money was like an incendiary to him, it would disappear in flames and burn him in the process, we might buy him a one-way ticket to Paris: just the ticket, so to speak. But first we should make sure this Shoshana actually wanted him there.

I call Shoshana in Paris. She is planning to leave shortly for the airport, to pick up my father. He's not coming, I tell her. She is alarmed, what's the matter, is he sick? No, he just didn't have the money for the ticket. No money? I thought he had money. I don't want him here without money; I can't take care of him. Well, my sisters and I will pay for his ticket. We just wanted to make sure he really had somewhere to go. No, no, no, don't send him here. Don't buy him the ticket.

Still, in his mind, he's convinced I will send him the check. The check, he tells everyone, is in the mail. On a certain Tuesday, he packs his suitcase, gets dressed, and sits and waits for the mail to come, and for Arnold to drive him to the airport. The check does not come. Jacquelyn calls me that night.

What can a daughter do to steer her father toward the right help? I am not a religious person, but since this feels like a Talmudic question, I would like to call up the old rabbis, all of them, and listen in while they take their time, across the centuries, to answer it. In looking for their advice, I come across Lesson 227 of Elu Metzios: (If he found) his own lost article and his father's lost article, the saving of his own lost article takes precedence; his own lost article and his Rabbi's lost article, his own takes precedence; his father's lost article and his Rabbi's lost article, that of his Rabbi takes precedence.

All those lost articles... Surely my father is a lost article, and surely I always feel lost. I had another dream last night about being lost, this one in the streets of Greenwich Village, but the streets were all mixed up, in the way dreams get things all wrong. I wandered the streets and climbed fire escapes up and down, lost, all the while carrying this piece of paper that was a French baby. I needed to find my way home where I had left a bag of peanuts to take to the zoo so that I could show this little piece of paper how to feed the elephants.

I tried to say to Arnold and Jacquelyn both: it may look to them like it should be a simple matter for us, the daughters, to take care of my father and relieve them from that burden, but it was not simple. Certainly it was also not up to them to care for him. I was sorry for them. I couldn't seem to explain so that they would understand. They didn't have the benefit of my lifetime of experience to know to say no to my father, even when he was at his most convincing, his most beguiling, his most pathetic, his most coercive, his most aggressive.

I did not send him the money for the ticket to Paris, but his ambition is still alive, he still sees a way out of the terror of New York, there's a painting he has in some storage facility, Sotheby's will auction it off for him, it's worth $20,000, there's some reparation check coming from Germany, supposed to go to his stepmother, but now it will go to him, $5,000, just a little delay due to the change in beneficiary—still he's scheming. But now—he doesn't know it yet—he has nowhere to land in Paris. Shoshana doesn't want him. What have I done?

Chanukah. *Borukh ate, singt der tate, un er tsind di likht. Un di shtraln milde faln oyf zayn blos gezikht.* Blessed are you, sings the father, and he lights the candles. And the mild rays fall on his pale face. What have I done? I spent my childhood loving my father, wanting to be like him, wanting to take care of him. He was so gentle. He was so mild, with his pale face and far-away eyes. His red hair, his freckles. The way he spoke, the accent which didn't sound like accent to me, but that no? rising after each thing he said: *n'est-ce pas?*, the taking back, the uncertainty, the asking for confirmation. He was so benign.

I wanted to be left-handed. I was six-and-a-half and I wanted to be different, and to be left-handed was to be different, I knew that. But now I think about it, it was about wanting to be like him. I wanted him. And I confused it with wanting to be like him. But maybe it's not a confusion. Maybe what you want when you want somebody is to be them in some way. Then if you are them, you have them. I wanted to be left-handed, I wanted to be French, I wanted him. I was six-and-a-half. I didn't want my mother, I wanted him.

I called Jacquelyn back, and said, sorry, Shoshana doesn't want him, and we are not sending him a ticket or any money. Sorry, sorry, you have to get him out of your place yourself. We will not come get him. Jacquelyn was pissed off, I could tell. And who wouldn't be?

My father managed to get a plane ticket to Paris from my mother's sister.

Another series of phone calls. The first came at four in the morning: a Parisian hotel clerk. The clerk wanted my credit card number in order to guarantee my father's hotel bill. My father had already run up quite a bill, and his own credit card appeared not to be good. My father assured the clerk he had a check waiting to clear at the bank, and that he would be able to cover the bill himself once it did. In the meantime, if I did not give the clerk my credit card number, he would be forced to ask my father to leave the hotel. It was February, and cold in Paris.

Was this actually a hotel clerk? Was it some friend or acquaintance my father had enlisted to get my credit card number, so he could use it to pay his way in Paris? I told the clerk I was not prepared to give him the number.

The second call came later that day, the same hotel clerk. If I didn't give him my credit card number, the hotel was going to call the police and they would put my father in jail for not paying his bill. I told him I wouldn't do it. Wait, he said, and then my father came on the phone, screaming at me. I'm not asking for money. Just give me the credit card number. You're going to let your father go to jail? Your father? This is the daughter I raised? I wish I could believe you, I said. I wish I could. But I don't trust you.

The next day a call came from the American Embassy in Paris. It was a woman's voice. I have your father here, she said. He needs money for a plane ticket back to New

York. He says he's a French citizen? She was puzzled. Yes, I said. He has dual citizenship. He was born in France. Well, he has a U.S. passport, and we're advising all U.S. citizens to leave France. There's a lot of anti-U.S. sentiment here with the war in Iraq. It's not safe for him to be here. I didn't know what to say. He needs money for a ticket back to New York, she repeated. I'm sorry, I said. I'm not going to pay for his ticket.

Two days later, a phone call from the hospitality desk at JFK airport in New York. Your father arrived from Paris last night, a woman said, and spent the night at the airport. He can't stay here. He says he has no money and no place to go, and that the U.S. Embassy paid for his plane ticket to New York. He gave me your phone number.

I imagined my father with his clothes disheveled, a stubby growth of beard on his face, hungry and cold, dirty, smelling. I'm sorry, I said. I don't know what you should do, but I can't come and get him.

Out my window, five deer stand very still in the field behind our house. What do the deer meditate on? Corn in the cornfield? Or is theirs a meditation not on desire but on fear, the hunter. Do they know the hunter if they've never experienced one? Or is there some kind of ancestral memory, genetically laid down; are they born with the knowledge of the hunter, passed on from one generation to the next without words?

This is the legacy I carry in me. My father did not pass it on through words, not that way, but in his very being, how he moves through the world, through life, through all his relationships, the way he does or cannot do or wants to do, the way he is. He could never talk about fear. All of his stories of being in Nazi-occupied France are strangely absent of fear, full of bravado. And I don't learn only from him; I learn also from his sister who calls us and talks and talks on the phone, talks for hours so my parents just leave the phone sitting there on the ledge in our kitchen, or propped up on the bed, and anyone of us can pick it up, listen to her going on and on—until eventually it is quiet and we hang the phone back up. It is the way she talks, the hoarse hysteria of her voice but also the fact that we never hang up on her. This is what is passed on to me, unspoken; as a child this is what I know.

We neither listen to her nor hang up.

My father went from JFK to the homeless shelter in the middle of a winter storm. Eight hundred-fifty beds, men only. There are about thirty-eight thousand people in New York City living in homeless shelters, most of them families with children.

At the age of forty-nine I seem to have acquired a brother. His name is Stanley Benjamin, or Benjamin Stanley. My father has used both versions when he talks about him. It was my father who arranged for us all to meet at a Greek restaurant not far from where he lives in a single-room-occupancy hotel on the Upper West Side of New York City.

The logistics were rather complicated, made the more so because my father has a little trouble with dates and times. He seems to do fine with locations. He knows who everybody is, although it has long been a problem (since we were kids) that he mixes up names very easily. My sisters lived much further away and, as it turned out, weren't able to come. I drove down from Northampton with my partner Mandy and our daughters, Tavi, ten, and Lili, seven. The last time we had seen my father was at my nephew's bar mitzvah, six years ago. At that time my father's drinking problem was quite bad. He almost fell off the bima when he went up for the aliyah, to chant the blessing for my nephew.

I had always wanted an older brother. I imagined he would teach me to play tennis, and bridge, and chess, and he would be very funny and play practical jokes on our parents. He would take me to the movies, and to ball games, and we would have a secret language that he made up and taught me, only me. I would be his favorite, of all his sisters. I once even told a friend of mine that I actually had an older brother who was in the army. Why the army? It is not like me to plan ahead and leave myself an out (killed in action) for when the brother never appeared.

And now Benjamin or Stanley has appeared. Although I'm not sure that he's older than me. But he acts like an older brother might. For one thing, he's very kind. I learned of his existence about six months before the lunch meeting, from my father and from my father's social worker, Ephraim Orlovsky.

Ephraim runs the Homelessness Prevention Program for an agency in New York City called Koved, which provides services to seniors. The homeless shelter my father went to after arriving at JFK hooked him up with Ephraim and the agency. Ephraim helped my father into a better homeless shelter, one just for seniors—much smaller and safer than the eight hundred fifty-bed men's shelter that he had been in—and then found a room for him in the SRO.

My father hates the hotel. It's one of the things he wanted to talk about at the Greek restaurant. Ephraim has helped my father get onto the list for section eight housing, although it could be a long wait for a studio apartment to open up, especially because my father refuses to live in any borough except Manhattan. In the meantime, the agency paired my father with a volunteer, what they call a "friendly visitor," and that is Stanley. Stanley and my father started meeting once a week about a year ago, and it has been working out so well that the agency is going to make a little video about the two of them. They plan to show it at training sessions for new volunteers. I guess you could say my father has become the poster boy for Koved. If they ever did a telethon, I bet they would invite him to appear.

Stanley is just what you would want for a brother. He's smart but not in the least arrogant; on the contrary, he's quite self-effacing. He works as an actuary for a life insurance company. My father had told me about his PhD from Princeton, but that turned out to be entirely my father's fantasy. It is true that Stanley is an actuary, and it's a coincidence that I was once an actuary, for a very short time when I first graduated from college. I guess it runs in the family!

We were the first to arrive at the restaurant. I stayed out on the sidewalk to wait for my father, while Mandy went inside with the girls to check out the menu and the seating. I kept looking in the direction he'd be coming from, scanning the crowds to see if I could spot him. I wasn't sure I would recognize him. The pictures I held of him in my mind would no longer be the right ones. For instance, playing tennis. The way he would switch the racquet from his left to his right hand to make the shot. The "Oy, Harry," when he missed. His face, always one eye half-shut, the eye on the side where his cigarette dangled, half-shut to block out the smoke. Even without a cigarette in his mouth, one eye was always squinting. His hands, of course, faint tufts of red hair on the backs of his fingers. His nails always impeccably clean. I used to watch him scrub them meticulously with a nailbrush every evening when he came home from work as a textile consultant in the garment district.

From about a block away I spotted him, unmistakably my father, walking slowly down the crowded street towards the restaurant. He looked small and old. His red hair had faded into a lighter orange, mixed with white. He seemed to concentrate with each step. Maybe his shoes were too big for him? He clutched a yellow envelope under one arm. As he approached, I could see that he wore several layers of mismatched shirts and sweaters under his jacket. I wondered where he got his clothes. My Daddy. He didn't see me until he got close. We hugged, and kissed three times, alternating cheeks, as is the French custom and was always his. His shave was uneven. He stepped back and looked at me. "Your hair is grey," he said, disapproving. I guess I looked old, too. His teeth didn't fit his mouth anymore, and when he spoke his speech was slightly slurred. Actually he sounded quite a lot the way he used to sound when he'd been drinking, but he wasn't drunk now. What surprised me was the realization that I didn't feel afraid of him, both because I didn't, and because I hadn't known that I had believed I would.

My daughters felt shy to meet my father, and we all seemed a little awkward until Stanley arrived. Clearly Stanley and my father were comfortable with each other. Stanley insisted that we didn't need to thank him for being such a good friend to my father. "It's mutual," he said. "I get as much from the friendship with your father as he does." He paused, adjusted his glasses with his middle finger and thumb. By the end of the lunch, this gesture felt so familiar it was as though I remembered him doing it when we were children together. "More than he does," he corrected himself.

I felt a hint of jealousy when he said this. Was it sibling rivalry already? Maybe not jealousy, but sadness. I wanted to ask Stanley, what was it he got from the relationship with my father? But my father was sitting right there, rifling through papers as he pulled them out of the worn yellow envelope. It was not a conversation I could have in front of him. Perhaps it was not a conversation I could have at all.

Here is the agenda my father set for our luncheon meeting: section eight housing, reparations money from Germany, rescuing items from storage, the building in East Berlin, how to retrieve messages from his cellphone. Also, introducing Stanley to the family.

I sat here very aware of the way my father kept poking his fingers inside his v-neck sweater to scratch his chest. I was thinking about bedbugs and wondering about responsibility. I reached to scratch my own left shoulder. I did greet my father with a hug. Was it possible that I now had bedbugs? I should not have read that article in the *New York Times* about the recent epidemic of bedbugs before we made the trip down here.

My father pushed his plate and glass toward the center of the table to make room for his papers. He began to speak. Soon an apartment in a section eight building on West Seventy-Third Street was to become available to him, he told us. He had become friends with the manager of the building, and she was going to put him in the apartment right next to hers because she liked him so much. As he spoke, I realized that my father lives in the near future, a near future of his imagining. The past held many misfortunes and much suffering, and the present was unbearable. But over the years the near future had proven to be the one place of hope and promise, the one place he had control over. When the apartment became available, he continued, his daughters would lend him money for furniture and a security deposit. He would pay his daughters back when the German government sent him the reparations check for $5000 that had been transferred to his name after his stepmother died. In addition, the German government would soon release the money that was coming to him from a building in East Berlin that his stepmother's grandfather had owned. Any day now, the necessary papers would be processed to authorize those funds. It would amount to two hundred thousand dollars. At that time, he would be able to pay off the storage company that was holding his last remaining possessions. His children would inherit the rest of the money after he died, and they would think back on him fondly as a generous and caring parent. One more thing. He needed an electric razor.

When I was studying French in high school, I once asked my father to teach me how to say one thing in

French the way it would be said authentically by a native French speaker. We landed on the phrase, "*mais tu sais bien, monsieur, que je n'ai pas de montre*" (but you know very well, sir, that I don't have a watch). As it turns out, my father and I would make one trip to France together, when I was in my thirties, so that I could finally meet my French cousins. He was drunk most of the time and was always disappearing to dip into a bar or liquor store. But once, while riding on the Metro, probably because he was trying to gauge how long it would be until we reached our stop and he could get a drink, he turned to me and asked, "What time is it?"

"*Mais tu sais bien monsieur que je n'ai pas de montre.*"

In the Talmud, in the section Elu Metzios, I found something interesting. The question is raised: if you find an object lying on the ground, when is it okay just to take it, and when must its discovery be announced? It is okay just to take the object if the previous owner has given up possession, but that raises the question of when can it be assumed that the previous owner no longer has possession? After much discussion and dissection of the question, having to do with what is found and where, the rabbis come to the following conclusion: at the moment the previous owner gives up hope of retrieving the lost object, that is when it no longer belongs to him.

It was because I lost the watch my father once bought me for my birthday that I stopped wearing a watch. Not that I had exactly worn it before then, but I had always carried it with me in my pocket. It was a plain watch, silver, with a black leather wristband. I never liked the feel of something around my wrist. I cried when I realized it was lost, after bicycling to work one summer when I was twenty. It must have fallen out of my pocket on the bike ride. I retraced the route, looking everywhere. No watch. And because I wanted *that* watch, I have never bought another one.

And my father? Whatever it is, however long it has been lost, what is once yours remains yours until you relinquish hope.

ASHES

The sky was still light and the air warm at 7 pm on the soft May evening when I turned into the driveway. I had made an appointment with the funeral director to pick up the ashes before going to my chorus rehearsal at the Jewish school nearby. I hesitated before unbuckling my seat belt. Was I going to cry?

From the outside, the funeral home looked like an ordinary, if somber, house: a brown Victorian with a black roof, and black shutters on all the windows. Heavy-leafed rhododendron bushes not yet in bloom added to the dark and claustrophobic feel. I followed the slate walkway up to the front door and rang the bell.

I was having misgivings, but it was obviously too late by now to do anything about it. As I stood waiting at the door, I recited to myself the advertising copy that I had apparently committed to memory: "Cremation is a green burial alternative. For those concerned about their final footprint, cremation is an environmentally friendly end-of-life choice." I pictured my father with his walker taking one last step before keeling over. His final footprint.

The question was: should I have arranged instead for a proper Jewish burial in a Jewish cemetery? With a rabbi? And kept his body intact? We had never discussed these alternatives while he still had his full cognitive capacities. Such as they were. I knew that he had been raised Orthodox and rejected the religion when fairly young. My family had not belonged to a synagogue. However, now I remembered that he had chanted the blessings without any trouble when he was called to the bima for my nephew's bar mitzvah (although my father had drunk so much, even that early in the day, that he stumbled on his way up the steps). Those prayers were in him. It was probably like riding a bicycle. But did that mean he would have liked to revert to tradition now that the end was near? The last time I rode a bicycle I went over the handlebars and landed on my face. Even when the ability to ride a bicycle is programmed in you, you still don't necessarily want to do it ever again. I would never know what he really thought.

We did have a conversation about it one of the times he had been taken to the hospital from the nursing home. Not the broken hip, nor the congestive heart failure, but the gastric bleed. While driving to see him at the hospital, imagining the worst, I decided that if he was not too far gone, I would ask him what he wanted after he died. Knowing of course that whatever he said, it would be unclear whether it was my father speaking or the dementia. At least I would have some information when it came time to decide.

They made me put on a gown and paper slippers over

my shoes and latex gloves before I entered his room since he had tested positive for some highly infectious bacteria—was it c-diff? They said it was hospital policy and it didn't mean that he was actually sick with it or contagious. "We all carry all kinds of bacteria all the time," the nurse explained. That was not reassuring, although it seemed it was intended to be. So I put on the protective gear and entered the room.

My father lay in the bed, attached to a blood pressure monitor and also an IV. A large man stood near him. I walked over and, hesitating only a bit because of the c-diff, kissed my father on both cheeks. His forehead seemed huge underneath the wisps of fading orange hair; his mouth was caved in because they had removed his dentures. He was wearing one of those little gowns and I couldn't help but notice that he had no underwear on. I tried not to look. "This is my daughter," my father said to the man.

The man, who was the gastroenterologist, introduced himself to me; we shook latex hands. "I'm glad you're here," the doctor said. "Your timing is good: I was just explaining the situation to your father."

"My daughter is a doctor." One might think my father said that because the doctor and I were dressed in identical gowns because of the c-diff, but in fact whenever I visited my father in a hospital, he always told everybody that I was a doctor, no matter what I was wearing.

The (true) doctor asked, "What's your specialty?"

I replied, "Actually, none—I'm not a doctor."

My father didn't believe me. "You're not? I thought you were a doctor."

"Well, sorry, Dad, you're wrong about that."

At that point the doctor asked me, in a suspicious tone, "Is he really French?" I confirmed that he was.

"*Mais oui*," My father turned toward the doctor. "See—I'm right about that."

"*Oui Papa, t'as raison. Bien sur*," I winked at him.

Then the doctor became business-like, and speaking now in a loud voice, the way people do who think someone with dementia will understand better if you speak louder, he launched into his explanation, which entailed a lot of multi-syllabic words including colonoscopy. He was asking my father's permission to perform one, but my father looked at me with a blank face, so I said (softly, because my father had excellent hearing), "Dad, they need to do a procedure to find out why you've been bleeding. It might be uncomfortable: do they have your permission?"

"Is it safe?" my father asked. I turned to the doctor—I always imagined myself as a simultaneous interpreter when with my father in the hospital. Not that he didn't speak perfect English, but not every doctor knew how to communicate with him. And my father was not always able to communicate either. Sometimes he couldn't find the right words, but what was worse was the possibility that he might say something that sounded completely plausible except it was in fact entirely false. The doctor, still in a loud voice, now answered my father's question about the safety of the colonoscopy, citing all kinds of data about the probabilities of a variety of elaborately described dangers, on his way to making the case that actually the risks were minimal. My father looked at me expectantly.

"It's quite safe," I said. Or if not a simultaneous interpreter, a subtitle-writer for a foreign-language film: it was one of those times when a character might speak for five minutes but the subtitle merely reads, "No, thank you."

"Yes," said my father, "I give my permission. He can do what he wants." The doctor described the necessary preparations and the timing. I turned to my father but before I could say anything he waved his hand in dismissal and said, "It's okay, whatever they have to do. So long as they don't cut me open."

"No, no surgery involved," the doctor said and began again to explain the procedure. Finally, he was done speaking and left the room.

"Smart guy," my father said. "At least he thinks so!" We shared a laugh.

"How're you feeling, Dad? Are you in pain? You look a little pale."

"Not too bad. Why are you wearing that... those..." he waved his hand at my outfit.

"It's just a precaution... they want to prevent germs from spreading."

"They're worried about your germs?"

"Not mine specifically." I didn't exactly want to say that it was his germs that were the problem. "It's a hospital... They just want to be safe."

He looked around the room, a well-appointed single in the new wing of the hospital. "It's an excellent hospital. Very nice. The best. My wife is one of the owners."

"Yes, it's very nice." I paused. He didn't have a wife, and if he did, she wouldn't own this hospital. Now was the moment, and I had no idea how to approach this delicate topic. Maybe the wife. "Dad, I wanted to ask you about something. Have you and your wife ever discussed... well, I just wondered... I don't know if you've thought about...

like, what you might want... I mean... I don't mean you have to decide right now, you have plenty of time, but just to start thinking about it... Like, some people might want to be cremated... and some might want to be buried... I just wondered... whether you have some idea of what you want." Could I be more indirect and inarticulate? I could not say the words "death," "die," or "dead."

"What I want?"

"Yes! Like what you want after, I mean when the time comes... whether you might want a cremation or..."

"You mean after I die? What I want when I'm dead?"

"Yes! Have you thought about that?"

"When I'm dead? I'll be dead! What do I care?"

"So it doesn't matter to you?"

"I just want... I want people... I want you... to... remember me."

"Of course I'll remember you, Dad. I'll always remember you."

"That's what I want."

An aide pushing a cart with supplies entered the room at that moment and apologized for interrupting—she just needed to clean up the bathroom. My father grinned at me as the aide made her way into the bathroom. "Nice," he leered with a toothless grin as he depicted a round shape with his two hands. I couldn't tell whether it was her breasts or her rear he was describing.

"Dad..." I gave a look of disapproval.

"I know, you think I'm terrible," he chuckled.

"Well..." He was right. I did think he was terrible. But to him it was a joke. I would remember him always and sometimes that was a problem. Sometimes I wished I could just forget him.

Finally, the door to the funeral home opened. I could spot the shiny black plastic box sitting on a doily on the front hall table. Like a tombstone, its height was its largest dimension, about ten inches. Mr. Pease was wearing the same brown suit and black tie that he had been wearing when I was there earlier in the week to make the arrangements and pay for the cremation. I realized now that he was dressed to match the house. Mr. Pease. Peas porridge hot. Peas porridge cold. Peas porridge in the pot, nine days old. I tried not to picture a nine-day-old corpse. I had liked him at the first meeting: he was calm and organized and although he seemed kind, he didn't say anything to me about being sorry for my loss. I appreciated that—he got right down to business and was efficient about it. And he never once used the word cremains. I hated that word. It sounded like something invented by an advertising company. Like when they intentionally used the wrong spelling: rite or nite. Actually, it sounded like some kind of breakfast cereal. One of those brands with too much sugar. Captain Crunch Cremains. The powdery stuff that was left in the bottom of the cereal box.

I liked Mr. Pease for calling them what they were: ashes. Tonight too, he was efficient. He had me sign two copies of the receipt, placed one on the table, the other in an envelope that he secured with a rubber band around the box of ashes. Then he handed me the box. "Here you are," he said. The transaction happened quickly; I didn't know what I had been expecting, but now here I was with this box. It was heavier than I had imagined. I did like the look and the feel of it: its smoothness and compactness and its rounded edges. I stood there, not quite able to move. I thought I might start to cry.

"Everything all right, then?" he asked. It seemed that he had something to do. Maybe there was a body waiting for him in the back room.

"Yes, good night. Thank you." I would likely never see Mr. Pease again in my life and that made me feel sad. I had found him comforting, and now I was on my own, with the box of ashes. And what would I do with these ashes?

I had been similarly comforted by the staff at the nursing home and their matter-of-fact way when I went back to collect my father's belongings the day after he died. His body had already been removed. A nurse and a couple of aides greeted me warmly and accompanied me into the room. They loved my father. I had never told the nurses or the rest of the staff much about his life before he arrived there. I had not wanted to prejudice them against him. It didn't feel fair. I knew this was the last stop for him and, although I hadn't precisely articulated it to myself, I felt protective of him—wanted to unburden him from his history. Of course, I couldn't prevent him from being himself. They came to know all the sides of him—his anger and stubbornness and refusal to cooperate, but also, once he had felt more comfortable there, his charm and sense of humor. And his flirtatiousness. His unbounded lust and preoccupation with sex. Which didn't bother them at all. Some of them seemed quite amused by it, in fact. Flattered, even. They enjoyed it because they felt safe.

Although I did witness that one time on my father's birthday when the nurse Jody, who had been his primary caretaker, gave him a birthday kiss on the cheek. When Jody stepped back after planting the kiss, my father leaned toward her again with a big smile, saying "The French way." Jody turned bright red and took another step back, flustered. I had to explain that what he meant by "the French way" was a kiss on each cheek. Such relief on Jody's face. She laughed. "I thought he meant—he was going to—"

"Yes, I could tell that's what you thought," I said.

Toward the end his fantasy life had become completely real to him. He didn't have access to alcohol and he didn't need it anymore. He sat in his chair by the open door of his room, watching the staff as they went about their tasks. Sometimes when I sat with him, he would point to a nurse or an aide and comment on her attractiveness, describing in detail how she had pleasured him during the night. He believed he was an important person living in some kind of high-class bordello, and all these women were there to service him, day and night.

And now he was dead. He came to the nursing home with virtually nothing and during the years there accumulated little: a few cards and photos that my sisters and I had sent or brought. A small CD player and a few CDs. Books, a deck of cards, a sketch pad and some colored pencils, none of which he had ever used. I would leave his clothes for another resident. Someone could surely use them. Mostly sweatpants and several soft cotton t-shirts. His sneakers were probably of no value to anybody. I had bought the pair and taken one of them to a cobbler for a lift when he broke his hip—his left leg was shorter after the surgery. His dentures had disappeared some months ago. And like the sneaker with the insert: what good would someone else's dentures have been to anybody? Would the crematorium have kept them in his mouth for the cremation if they had been found? Burning plastic? That could be toxic. Better this way. The only item that really felt meaningful was a pair of sunglasses. He rarely went outside, but his eyes were often sensitive even to indoor light, and he liked to wear sunglasses. They made him look very hip. Or like he was in the Mafia. Inexpensive glasses from CVS. I had bought several replacement pairs during the years that he was there—somehow he managed to lose them, or maybe another resident would walk off with them. But this last pair I would keep. My inheritance. That's what it came down to—a pair of sunglasses. I cried as I hugged these caring nurses and assistants good-bye. I would probably never see them again. I had not anticipated all the smaller good-byes that were embedded in the bigger good-bye. Some people I didn't really know at all and had never met. Like the Comcast person who I spoke to on the phone about closing his cable account. Such a kind and understanding woman. I even shed a tear for her when we hung up.

I found myself wishing I had told the caregivers at the nursing home just how bad things had been for him—and for me—before he arrived there. I had a strong desire to tell them all the things I had never before disclosed. This had been the chance, and I didn't do it. Did I want something from them for myself? It was very confusing. And now it was too late.

I opened the back door of my car and cradled the box of ashes in my arms before placing it down, careful to lean it against the seat back so it wouldn't tip over. For a brief moment the thought flitted through my mind that I should fasten the seatbelt over the box. I had an image of the cushioned child safety seat we had used when our kids were young. The black box would have fit well in it. I imagined securing the box in the car seat with its child-sized buckle. And as I drove to the Jewish school, I was aware that I was going more slowly than usual, taking particular care at each stop sign or traffic light, or when making a turn, as I had done when I first became a mother and drove with my baby in the car. That same feeling of protectiveness. Although, truly, he was dead already, so what did it matter?

I was early for rehearsal and didn't want to go in just yet. Curious to look at the ashes, I got out of the car and went around to sit in the back, pulling the box onto my lap. The top had a simple clasp like that of a box of diaper wipes; all I had to do was push it up with my thumb and it opened to reveal a black plastic bag fastened with a twist tie. I removed the tie and peered inside the bag. Greyish ash. Light grey. Like sand, with some bigger chunks. A heap of sand, as in the Sorites paradox, the paradox of the heap. If you remove one grain of sand from a heap, you still have a heap. Another grain, still a heap. And if you kept doing that? At the end you would be left with just one grain of sand. Surely that is no longer a heap. So when did the heap cease to become a heap?

At rehearsal I fought back tears. All those Jewish songs in minor keys. I had heard that when you're about to die, your whole life flashes before you. I had no idea whether that was true and how anyone could possibly know it if, in fact, it was. But now it seemed to me that because my father had died, my own life was flashing through my head. That's how it felt.

It was my partner Mandy and I who had cleared out his room in the Single Room Occupancy Hotel five years earlier when we drove down to New York City to fetch him. His room smelled of feces and of urine—like he'd been living in a cage at a zoo with no keeper. According to the social worker there, his passport and all other documents had been stolen by a prostitute that he had invited up to his room. I had hoped to find something, anything that might have told me something I didn't already know about his life or who he was. Or something that might have had meaning for him. But all I found were some old clothes and papers. The clothes that he could still use we put in a trash bag to take with us—I'd let the nursing home laundry wash them. We scooped up whatever papers were lying around, but when I went through them there was nothing that meant anything anymore. Correspondence with a lawyer about making a claim on his stepmother's interest in a building in Berlin that the Nazis had seized. My father had been obsessed with that project—he felt sure he had about $200,000 coming to him—but the lawyer's letters were unequivocal. My father had missed some deadline and there would be nothing. Nothing. Another letter—this one from the storage company where he had rented a container for his furniture and paintings after he was evicted from his last apartment. He had always talked about one particular painting he claimed was worth $50,000. This letter was a final notice—informing my father that they were selling all his possessions. I remembered that day when my father called me and asked me to contact the storage place. I had phoned them, only to learn that it had been six months since he had sent in a payment and they had mailed a dozen notices and now it was too late to retrieve anything of his—they had already sold or disposed of it all. Sorry. There was nothing they could do about it.

This had been my father's usual way. He had lived a life of missed deadlines. And I was afraid that would be true for me, too. How hard it sometimes was to get things done. I thought that nobody who knew me would guess how difficult the requirements of living in the world felt to me. As they had been for him.

For a moment as I approached the car after rehearsal, I actually believed that my father was in the car. That's how it felt—that my father himself was sitting there in the back seat, waiting for me to drive him home. Not his ashes, but him. My actual father. He had been sitting there amusing himself while happily, patiently, waiting for my rehearsal to end before I drove him home. To my home.

"So Dad, my rehearsal's over and I'm gonna take you home now. To my house." I buckled myself in. Actually, it felt nice not to be alone. "Do you want to listen to the radio?" I fiddled with the dial. I knew that reduced to his ashes he was not still a person, but at the same time he was not *not* a person, and I enjoyed the warm feeling of his companionship. "OK Dad, anything particular you want to listen to? What are you in the mood for? Classical? Top 40's? Jazz? Oldies?"

I want to hold your ha-a-a-a-annnnd.

"Oldies it is. You've always enjoyed the Beatles." Then without warning, I felt a sudden stab of fear at the thought of bringing my father home with me. I had never allowed my father into my home. Especially after I had daughters of my own. He could not be trusted.

It had been a shock to my system when I even considered bringing him up to the Care Center—the nursing home nearby—to live so close to me. And then I actually decided to do it. The first few weeks after he arrived at the nursing home I felt as though I couldn't breathe. Why had I done this? My beautiful life, with Mandy and the kids, was it going to end? Would there ever be space from him in my thoughts? Would I ever again have a day where I could just go about my life without suddenly remembering—oh, my father—he's right here. In my town. Every time I drove past the Care Center on my way to mail something, or to pick something up at CVS— it was a sudden jolt. There he was, my father, in that building. Why had I done it?

Because I had to do something. He was in bad shape— dementia on top of the alcohol and the bipolar diagnosis— and he could no longer live on his own. The choices were a nursing home in New York or a nursing home near here. I had imagined the next few years with him in a nursing home in New York City. What if something came up? What if he had to go into the hospital? It would be much easier with him nearby. That was the rational reason. But not the only reason. Somewhere inside me I had not let go of the hope that these last years of his life might offer some chance of... of what? Of having my father again? In spite of his past: his drinking, his unchecked sexuality, his rage that occasionally exploded in bursts of violence, his lies, the late-night desperate, angry phone calls asking me for money—in spite of all of that, was it possible that my old father—the gentle father I had adored when I was very young—was still in there somewhere and would re-emerge? At some point my father became not my father. But I never stopped longing for the father that had disappeared. And never stopped hoping that he would return.

As frightened as I was once he moved to the Care Center, and in spite of years of resolve to keep him out of my home, once he was so close by I found myself fantasizing about picking him up and bringing him back to my house for a little visit. After all, a nursing home was not a prison. People who lived there were allowed to leave for a few hours, weren't they? Surely other families brought their parents home for an occasional visit. I had tucked that thought away.

It never happened. I had never brought him to my home, and I had never brought my children to visit him.

A few days before he died, he lay in bed, with a tube of oxygen feeding into his nose. He struggled for breath—was barely able to speak. I pulled a chair up next to his bed, and sat there, holding his hand, his skin very soft. His face was pale, his once orange hair almost completely white. When I was a child, we had sometimes sat together simply holding hands. I did believe there was a time when things had been easy. Now I sat beside him for a long time and when it looked like he had fallen asleep, I tried to unclasp his hand. He wouldn't let go. He clutched my hand tight, with surprising strength. "Okay, Dad," I said. "I guess you just want to hang onto me. That's okay, you hang on."

"I want to hang onto you always," he had said.

"I want to hold your hand. And when you touch me I feel happy, inside. It's such a feeling that my love, I can't hide. I can't hide. I can't hide..."
Singing along to the Beatles, I began to cry. I couldn't help it. I had loved him. In spite of everything he had done,

I had. It was that simple. So then, where could I put him? So that he would be safe. And so that I would be safe.

I turned into our driveway, the headlights casting skeletal shadows on our house, and pulled up beside the shed. Could I put the box of ashes in the shed? No, not in the shed, where we had to keep a bungee cord on the lid of the trash can so squirrels wouldn't get into it. And not in the basement, either, where there was evidence of mice. The thought of a squirrel or a mouse, chewing a hole through the box and then through the plastic bag, sniffing around the ashes, nibbling on the chunks of bone—depositing little droppings. No, that would be terrible. Not that I hadn't at times felt my father deserved an ending like that. Would I just have to leave him in the car? That wasn't right either. I did not want to take him with me everywhere I went. I wanted to be free of him.

When I had thought about cremation, I had imagined scattering a portion of his ashes in every place that he had lived. How better to mark his life? First Pabianice, the small town in Poland outside of Lodz where generations of his family had lived—my father had spent a couple of summers there as a young child before the war began; then Paris, where he was born, where he still had cousins, and where he had returned briefly toward the end of his life before everything fell apart; next Villars-sur-Ollon, Switzerland, where he had gone to boarding school for a few years as a child while his family was in Paris; then Nice, France, where his family spent a year after fleeing occupied France and before securing passage to the U.S.; Barcelona; Lisbon; Havana—the stopping points, one month each in Spain and Portugal, and three months in Cuba, on the way to New York City where he and his family finally settled. But always with an eye toward Europe. Recapitulating his life with his ashes. Would I actually manage to visit all those places?

In any case, in the meantime I would have to put the box somewhere in the house itself. Could I tolerate his presence in my house? Not in the center of things. Not in plain sight. And it went without saying, not in anyone's bedroom. It was a problem for so much of my life: what to do with my father? It was a big problem while he was alive, and now that he had died it was again a problem.

I had a friend who kept her mother's ashes on the mantelpiece over her fireplace. We had a fireplace. With a mantelpiece. But a mantelpiece felt so central. Although in our house it was not as though we used the fireplace for anything; we never made a fire because wood smoke gave me asthma. In fact, we had put the piano—a baby grand that had belonged to Mandy's mother—in front of the fireplace. We were that certain we would never build a fire in it. But whether we used the fireplace or not, I could not imagine his ashes right up there on the mantelpiece... they would be too visible.

I understood now the real reason why the Jewish tradition insisted that every piece of the body be bound up and placed in a casket with the whole thing buried somewhere in a cemetery under the ground. A year of mourning and then it was over. All those Jewish burial societies. It seemed to me that the real reason had nothing to do with the safekeeping of the soul of the person who had died or ensuring that their memory lived on. Not at all. It was to protect the people who remained alive. So that they didn't have to live with the dead person always, and constantly remember them. Make sure to gather up every piece of the body—so that nobody had to worry about some stray piece coming to haunt them when they didn't want it. Put the body in the ground—so that it wasn't right there in your house. So you could get a break from it—keep it outside the daily course of your life. Make a ritual so that the dead person's family could say a full goodbye. And then make sure it was a goodbye. And move on. Allowing, of course, for regularly scheduled (but infrequent) moments to honor the dead by saying Kaddish.

Perhaps I had thought I would free myself of my father's body—the body that had felt so threatening—by incinerating it. But to rid oneself of someone's body was not as simple as that. Corporeality persists in the mind even after the actual body has been disposed of. And now I had these ashes.

Well, then, why not in the fireplace itself? A great idea! Ashes to ashes. The box would be unobtrusive if it was tucked into the fireplace. I would not have to see it. I might sometimes remember he was there but could also easily forget.

And if I put the box near the piano, I could finally give my father a little bit of what I had been unable to give him when he was alive. From within the fireplace my father could listen to our daughter Lili practicing the piano. Lili had been taking piano lessons for years. He would like that. And I would like to do that for him. I thought he might be happy in the fireplace. And me? Perhaps with him safely hidden away, I could get on with my life.

I retrieved the box of ashes from the back seat and walked slowly toward my house. The light was on upstairs in our bedroom—probably Mandy was reading in bed.

Lili's bedroom light was off—she would already be in bed, if not asleep. Our older daughter Tavi was away at college. As I approached the front door I pictured in my mind exactly what I would do. I would open the door very quietly, walk directly back to the living room, crawl under the piano and place the box of ashes safely in the left corner of the fireplace behind the glass enclosure. And then I would whisper some words to him. What should I say? Maybe just goodbye. And I would tell him that I loved him. *Au revoir, mon père. Je t'aime.*

ACKNOWLEDGMENTS

Thank you to all lesbians and queer and trans people everywhere, for coming out and making this world a better place. Thank you to the city of Northampton where I had the good fortune to be living when I came out as a lesbian. Special thanks to the Mary Vasquez Softball League and my team Red Scare, and to the Northampton Gay and Lesbian Liberation March, which has continued in its many iterations to the present day.

Thank you to the Bennington Writing Seminars and to my skillful teachers Betsy Cox, Alice Mattison, Lynne Sharon Schwartz, and Askold Melnyczuk. I am especially grateful to Alice for your belief in me and for our continuing relationship. Thank you to my fellow students, especially E. Louise Beach, Ilina Singh, Sandra Worsham, Dick Gotti, and Dave Kalish.

Dick and Dave, I cannot thank you enough: without you this book would not exist.

Thank you to all the people at Atmosphere Press, especially my editor Alexis Kale for your encouragement and valuable suggestions.

Thank you to my mother Henny Philips for your love of books, for the example of your rich friendships, and for your understanding; to my father Henri Dabek for all that I learned from you about compassion and forgiveness; to my sister Ruth Hoffman for your empathic response to my writing; to my sister Lisa Dabek for all that we have shared and for what you give to my children; and to my aunt, Sheila Oaks Horwitz, for the loving late night talks, for the summer I lived with you, and for showing me what a life spent pursuing one's passion can look like.

Thank you to the places that sustain me: The Common School library and the school's great teachers and staff; The Jones Library in Amherst; The Wellfleet Public Library; The Literacy Project and its amazing students; Baystate Hospital's NICU, its dedicated staff and the brave and beautiful babies; The Emily Dickinson Trail; Mt. Norwottuck; Rattlesnake Knob; Great Island; Duck Harbor; and the ocean beaches along the tip of the Outer Cape.

Thank you to all my wonderful friends whose love, support for my writing, and presence in my life mean everything to me: Susan Barkan, Eileen Barry, Alison Bechdel, Bob Berk, Brian Berk, Bunny Berk, Amy Brodigan, Leish Clancy, Faith Conant, Sheryl Derderian, Pat DeAngelis, Wraye Dugundji, Jan Eidelson, Jean Esther, Barbara Findlen, Kristen Golden, Jennifer Holme, Jana Jagendorf, Christopher Janeway, Becky Jones, Kate Lamdin, Catherine Leiser, Karen Levine, Carol Lewis, Maya Rege-Colt, Jean Meister, Marcia Merithew, Jaime Michaels, Robyn Miller, Linda Morgenstern, Leslie Morris, Catherine Newman, Sue Pearce, Johanna Plaut, Cindy Probst, Judy Raiffa, Elaine Riley, Craige Roberts, Nancy Salzer, Macci Schmidt, Hannah Schwarzschild, Pengy Shannon-Dabek, Judy Stern, Marilyn Stern, Janet Surrey, Cindy Turnbull, Arinna Weisman, Liz Welsh, Laura Wenk, Katy Winn-Ritzenberg, Marci Yoss, and Susan Zarchin.

Thank you most of all to my partner Peggy and our daughters Nadja and Eva, for all the ways in which you have supported my writing, and for filling my life with love and a joy I never could have imagined.

ABOUT ATMOSPHERE PRESS

Atmosphere Press is an independent, full-service publisher for excellent books in all genres and for all audiences. Learn more about what we do at atmospherepress.com.

We encourage you to check out some of Atmosphere's latest releases, which are available at Amazon.com and via order from your local bookstore:

Saints and Martyrs: A Novel, by Aaron Roe

When I Am Ashes, a novel by Amber Rose

Melancholy Vision: A Revolution Series Novel, by L.C. Hamilton

The Recoleta Stories, by Bryon Esmond Butler

Voodoo Hideaway, a novel by Vance Cariaga

Hart Street and Main, a novel by Tabitha Sprunger

The Weed Lady, a novel by Shea R. Embry

A Book of Life, a novel by David Ellis

It Was Called a Home, a novel by Brian Nisun

Grace, a novel by Nancy Allen

Shifted, a novel by KristaLyn A. Vetovich

Because the Sky is a Thousand Soft Hurts, stories by Elizabeth Kirschner

ABOUT THE AUTHOR

Nina Dabek has an MFA from the Bennington Writing Seminars. Her short films *Seth's Aunts* and *Searching for the Contact* screened internationally and on PBS and her short story *GRE* appeared in the *Milo Review*. A staged reading of her full-length play *Invitation to the Dance*, in collaboration with the Northampton Play Incubation Collective, is forthcoming. She lives in Amherst, MA with her partner. They have two daughters.